Rule # 3 Dad Knows Best

Rule # 3 Dad Knows Best

A SWEET, SMALL-TOWN COWBOY ROMANCE

RULES FOR DATING A SINGLE DAD

E.B. SILVA

Rules for Dating a Single Dad Series

The Rules for Dating a Single Dad series is a collection of 14 heartwarming sweet romance stories about single dads who discover that love doesn't follow a rulebook.

Featuring popular tropes such as fake relationships, friends to lovers, grumpy / sunshine, found family, opposites attract, love at first sight, and so much more!

Each story in Rules for Dating a Single Dad celebrates the unique journey of finding love as a single parent, proving that sometimes the most beautiful love stories include Legos and soccer games.

Rules for Dating a Single Dad—where touching family moments and heartwarming connections intersect with the magic of finding unexpected love!

CHECK OUT THE REST OF THE SERIES HERE

Chapter One

NAOMI

Heart's Desire Ranch lives up to its name. Decked out in glowing tea lights, the massive Great Room is a smaller version of Yellowstone National Park's Old Faithful Lodge, with no attention to detail spared. Dimmed lights and romantic country music provide the perfect vibe as Luna and Ledger twirl around the dance floor, the most inspiring, beautiful couple I've ever had the chance to know.

Luna's been my BFF since beauty school. But seeing her with her very attentive bridegroom puts a thick knot in my throat. So does the bridal bouquet I hold in my hand.

It figures that I would end up with it. Luna was obvious about calculating its trajectory with her eyes before turning and throwing the gorgeous bouquet of red roses into the air. Ten-year-old Maddie, the adorable daughter of the ranch's owners, Chanel and Chase, gave catching it a good try. Somehow, though, it still ended up with me despite my nonchalant attempts to shrug off the whole thing.

Fortunately, the tradition ended there. I've never been a big fan of the man who catches the bride's garter putting it on the leg of the woman with the bride's bouquet. It's always seemed a little chauvinistic to me. It helps that the garter catcher, Randall "Rugged" Collier—the epitome of tall, dark, and handsome—clearly only has eyes for Portia, a pretty single mom who traveled to this event with her son, Gregory. He's Maddie's age.

"I could've caught it if I wanted to, you know," a lazy Texas drawl says next to me. I look up into the face of the man I've exchanged glances, texts, and plenty of flirtatious words with all week. Nash Carter. Nevertheless, in all the wedding bustle, this stands to be our first conversation of any great length.

One look from the gorgeous cowboy and my pulse pounds, cheeks flush, and throat thickens with anticipation. But he's got bad boy written all over him, from his cocky lopsided grin to his irresistible dimples. He's the last thing a girl like me needs. I finger the chastity ring I wear on my left hand.

Nash's eyes tick to the shiny silver reminder. "I've been meaning to ask all week. That's not an engagement ring, is it?"

All week? Why does this confession make me flush with happiness? Swallowing loudly, I reply, "No, it's a purity ring."

"Ohh," he says, a mixture of relief and confusion flooding his face.

"What?"

"Nothing. Heard about those before but never seen one up close. Why did you make that decision?"

My face heats at the intimate inquiry. "Because it's what God requires and what I want. To be pleasing in the Almighty's sight, and to find one man to commit to for life."

He levels his eyes on mine. "Does that mean you're looking for a man who's made the same commitment to purity?"

The corners of my mouth uncontrollably turn up, and my

cheeks burn. "Not necessarily. But I'm looking for someone dedicated to God, marriage, and family."

"Even if that dedication came in a roundabout way?" he presses, narrowing his gaze on me.

I shrug. "I guess you could put it that way."

"Well, okay then," he replies, looking too relieved for me to ignore. It makes my heart skip inside my chest.

One of the ranch hands, Nash has acted as my main contact for wedding-related stuff, from arranging transportation from Montrose Regional Airport to Ouray for guests arriving at various times to running errands, helping with decorations, and leading dude ranch-style tours and horseback excursions.

We've communicated mainly through texts and very brief dialogues. But whenever we stand in the same room, the air feels thick enough to cut because of the wild chemistry darting back and forth between us.

"Nice to finally converse with the cowboy who acted as my Girl Friday this week," I tease, and he grabs my hand, shaking it before I can react.

"Girl Friday? No, ma'am. More like your devoted servant." His hand dwarfs mine, rough and work-hardened. The sparks darting back and forth between our eyes somehow condense and combine in his touch, making my heart race and my body warm. When he lets go, my hand feels inexplicably cold.

My throat tightens, and I work to swallow the lump that forms, saying, "Are you enjoying your small respite before all the chauffeuring begins again?"

He nods, clenching his jaw and narrowing his eyes. There's something so familiar about his face, but I can't quite place it. "Sure am," he drawls. "I've been meaning to ask but not wanting to get too personal. Do I detect a little Okie in your voice?"

"Sure do, though I'd say it's more like a lot."

"Yes, ma'am," he eyes me like he's not quite sure what to make of me. "It didn't come through in your texts."

"Neither did that hefty dose of Texas in yours."

He nods, running his fingers through his hair. "Guilty as charged."

"Going back to the beginning of our conversation, what is it that you're so sure you would have caught?"

"Why, the garter, of course."

I frown, scrutinizing his handsome bearded face and thick chestnut-colored hair. His jade-hued eyes snap with a mischievous wittiness that looks like he's got something amusing to say, although whatever it is, he doesn't share.

"But you didn't catch it, which tells me all I need to know about you."

"And what's that?" he asks, amusement written on his face.

"Bad-boy cowboys. You're all the same. Getting one of you to settle down is like trying to lasso a tornado."

He chuckles, a deep, resonant sound that makes my cheeks heat, though I don't know why. "Sounds like you've got me all figured out. Single for the long haul. But can I tell you a secret?"

He leans closer as if he's about to whisper in my ear.

"Sure," I say in whispy tones.

"Once I asked around and learned there would be no placing the garter on the leg of the bouquet catcher, I figured, what was the point?"

I blush, smiling broadly and uncontrollably at the handsome cowboy. "No point at all, in your case. I'd imagine."

He arches an eyebrow. "I'll admit I've been more of a rambler than most. But I'm a changed man, looking for a changed life."

The last sentence piques my curiosity, but I don't know if

I want to go there with him. Especially since I'm still trying to ascertain how sincere he really is.

Instead, I observe, "Most cowboys are ramblers in my experience. Of course, this place has many exceptions. Like Randall, I'd imagine, and definitely, Chase and Ledger."

"There's also Eldon." Nash nods toward the ranch foreman with his extravagant handlebar mustache. He stands in one of the corners, talking to Véronique, the ranch's cook. I've gotten the feeling they're together all week, and, by the looks of it, enjoying each other's company. The lovely French woman covers her face with her hands, blushing as the elder cowboy leans a little closer, looking like he's mid-joke.

"Maybe," I reply. I eye him curiously, feeling my cheeks burn some more.

Nash stands a good six foot three or four with a lean, muscular build. He keeps his brown beard well-trimmed and his hair short and clean-cut. His square, angular face showcases a strong chin, and his eyes glow in the dim light of the room, the prettiest shade of green I've ever seen, framed by thick, full lashes. Everything about him, from his sculpted lips to his well-proportioned, straight nose, exudes masculinity.

"Why maybe?" He chuckles, nodding towards Eldon.

"Well, I don't see a ring on it. Do you?"

"Shoot, girl, you mean business."

"Have to with cowboys," I tease, side-eyeing him.

"What do you have against cowboys?" he asks.

I shrug. "Not one thing in particular, but I grew up around them. So, I have a decent handle on their tendencies, tricks, and pickup lines."

"No tricks or pickup lines here. But how do you feel about dancing?"

My heart skips for like the millionth time since first seeing this man. "I thought you'd never ask."

"Is that a *yes*, darling?" He looks pleased as punch.

I nod more enthusiastically than I mean to, laughing under my breath and adding, "But please don't darling me—"

He shrugs. "Alright, you caught me."

"Unlike you and that garter," I quip.

"I should know better than to go near you Okie girls. Your brains are always going a million miles a minute, looking for ways to trip up poor, hapless stablehands."

I nod, feeling sparks run up and down the lengths of my arms as he faces me, offering his right hand and pulling me a hair's breadth closer to palm my lower back with his left. I let out an involuntary sigh, and he smiles. A dangerous kind of smile. All big, straight white teeth and two adorable dimples that beg me to kiss them.

Absolutely not, Naomi! This man's a walking red flag.

The opening strains of Luke Combs's "Forever After All" fill the room, and I give the thirty-something, long-haired DJ a dirty look.

"What are you scowling for?" Nash asks, raising his eyebrows. "You don't like Luke Combs?"

"On the contrary, I love this song. Just not for this dance."

"And why not?" he asks with a bad-boy chuckle.

Because I already like you more than I should. Don't need romantic crooners to help these feelings along any.

Instead of speaking my mind, though, I bite my tongue, trying not to let my eyes wander into his gaze again where they like to get hopelessly lost. The way he looks at me makes my insides feel warm and gooey. Time for a change of subject. "I've been meaning to ask you all week. You look familiar, Nash. Where do I know you from?"

"Apart from this week, I dunno. I'm new to Ouray by way of the Texas Hill Country. Bandera, to be exact. You might know it?"

I shake my head.

"Well, dar—I mean Naomi, you know less about cowboys than you let on."

"And why's that?"

"Because Bandera's the cowboy capital of the world."

"Is that right? Leave it to Texans to think they've got a monopoly on cowboys, too," I retort, shaking my head.

"You're full of an awful lot of opinions for such a petite woman," he mutters sarcastically, but a smile twinkles in his eyes.

"The understatement of the year, but I suppose it's a compliment, so I'll take it."

Nash counters, his face growing serious. "That's an observation, not a compliment."

"Well, then, what would a compliment be, cowboy?" I ask, kicking myself the moment the flirtatious words leave my mouth. The last thing I want is to encourage smooth-talking overtures from this cocky guy.

He leans a little closer, dropping his voice and mesmerizing me with his gorgeous green eyes. "A compliment would be me telling you you're the most beautiful woman in this room. The kind of beautiful that puts an ache in a man's chest that never goes away."

My face flushes, and the room suddenly feels scorching. But as a girl from Oklahoma who's heard it all before, I remain skeptical. Clearing my throat and trying to keep it together, I question, "Is that what you say to all the ladies?"

"What do you think?" he mutters gruffly.

"I don't know you well enough to make a judgment," I answer more breathlessly than I mean to. But I tell myself it's been a long day. I have every right to feel exhausted and even a little hazy, wrapped in a handsome cowboy's embrace or not. Scrunching my forehead and stiffening to put an almost imperceptible distance between us, I change the topic. "I'm almost certain of it. I've seen you somewhere."

He shrugs. "Rodeoing, maybe?"

I chuckle. "Oh no. I'm not from around here or Texas, as you already figured out from my accent."

"I don't mean local rodeos," he counters. "Until recently, I was one of the top saddle bronc riders in the Professional Rodeo Cowboys Association."

"The PRCA? Well, that makes sense," I exclaim, taking a small step back to stare at him. "My dad loves watching that stuff. I knew you looked familiar."

"Yep," he says, looking down. It's not the response I expect from a man like him.

"No bragging? No celebrating your fame and wins? You don't seem like the type of man who talks about fame without exploiting it."

"I'm sorry if I've given you that impression, ma'am. But I'm no braggart, and honestly, with how things ended, I don't have much to brag about."

"Oh," I exclaim, eyeing his somber face. His roguish good looks naturally go with a smile and a jovial personality, which makes his current mood feel awkward, like an ill-fitting jacket.

I ask, "Do you want to talk about what happened?"

He shrugs. "Not much to tell. Big injuries precipitated one of my worst years ever. Bad enough to throw me off the circuit for good."

"Injuries? Are you okay?"

"I'll spare you the details when it comes to what I feel like when I wake up in the morning. Suffice it to say, though, the most bruised part of me remains my ego."

"I understand," I say with a sympathetic smile. His face tightens ever so slightly with something akin to disbelief. So, I elaborate, "This past winter, Luna and I came to Ouray for a winter vacation. We rented cross-country skis and snowshoes for a week of outdoor fun. Only I had to severely break my left ankle."

"Ouch," he says, listening intently.

"It's why I'm not in heels," I add, looking down at my red flats. "When I say I broke my ankle, this wasn't some little wear-a-cast-for-six-weeks thing. Poor Luna had to call 911, and they sent out search and rescue to get me. I had a compound fracture, which traumatized Luna and meant surgery in Montrose followed by months of recovery. I had to relearn how to walk again and everything."

"No kidding?" He eyes my ankles.

I turn my left leg towards him and lift my red evening gown slightly so he can see the angry scar running up the side of my leg. He winces, making a hissing sound as he sucks air between his teeth.

"I ended up with a dozen screws and two plates to stabilize a broken tibia, shattered fibula, and dislocated ankle."

"Shoot, girl. You said Luna was traumatized, and you weren't? How is that possible?"

I cock my head to the side, measuring my words. "That's a good question. I grew up on a farm with baby goats and horses. So, I had to get over my gore issues early to help with births and all of that."

"But the pain?" he urges, clearly a man well-acquainted with the subject.

"Fortunately, I was surrounded by a massive natural ice pack with snow all around me. It kept my ankle somewhat numbed."

"Dang, woman, you're tough as nails."

I nod.

"And a country girl, to boot."

I shrug. "I told you I've been around cowboys my whole life. That said, our home was outside of Oklahoma City, so only farm-ish. But I'm in the California Bay Area now, which means big city all the time."

"Is that how you like things?"

"The Bay Area has delish food, wonderful shopping, and an endless array of performances and sporting events. Unfortunately, I'm not really into those things. I'd much prefer moving out here by Luna if I could find a decent job."

He laughs. "Choosing a small town over a big city? You're not like other girls."

"Maybe I am. Maybe I'm not. Do you have something against big-city girls?"

"Not at all. Big-city girls, small-town girls, and girls in general are among my favorite people. Especially after living in stinky, dirty, male-dominated ranch bunkhouses."

A surge of jealousy grips me, and I frown, though I don't know why. It's not my business who he sees, after all.

"And yet, you remain adamantly committed to the single life?"

"It's not about commitment..." He pauses, searching for the right words. "When I started working here, Eldon made me swear I would avoid drama, especially of the female persuasion. And I aim to do that."

"You like your job that much?"

He shakes his head. "The job's fine. But it's really a means to an end."

Curiosity piqued again, I take the bait. "What do you mean?"

"Owning my own ranch. It'll be a lot more modest than this place. After all, with Telluride right around the corner and so many movie stars living here, real estate prices are downright ridiculous. But a small operation like Ledger's wouldn't be half bad. And I can breed and train horses, too. I'm fantastic with equines. It's people who challenge me."

"Sounds like the perfect life for you."

"How about you? What's your plan for the future?"

I shrug. "Honestly, it's not so different from yours. I'd like to breed and raise alpacas and goats like my parents. Of course,

I'll keep chickens, too. So, kind of a homesteading operation with a wool production element."

"What's so special about alpacas and goats?" he puzzles.

"Alpacas produce the softest wool. It's perfect for my knitting side hustle. And goats? I just love them. Have you ever seen a baby goat before?"

"Of course."

I shake my head. "I mean a miniature baby goat. I can tell by your answer you haven't."

"Maybe not, then."

I reach for my purse, ready to pull out my phone and search for images. The volume of the DJ's music keeps rising, and the room feels hot, so I ask, "Want to head outside for a little fresh air?"

Nash's face relaxes, and he pulls on the collar of his dress shirt, unbuttoning the top. "Thank goodness you asked. It's miserable in here."

Chapter Two

NASH

Eldon's voice rings in my head as I turn, my left hand still palming Naomi's back as I lead her toward the front door. *Whatever you do, I expect no trouble or drama from you, especially of the female persuasion.*

He said this just the other day in a speech to the whole bunkhouse before the wedding. I thought obeying would be simple enough until my first sight of Naomi. Fortunately, the ranch foreman's too busy with the French cook to pay us any attention.

Outside, the chill of a May evening at high elevation feels refreshing, and we both sigh in relief.

"This is so much better," the sunshiny Okie says as I lead her towards a bench under a grouping of aspen trees a little ways down the expansive white gravel driveway on the lawn. The white rocks glow as if reflecting the heavenly astronomical display overhead.

"Yes, it is. You read my mind in there ... again. It was far too hot and loud for me."

We sit, and I look up at the night sky, exhaling as she rifles through her purse, pulling out her phone. They don't make nights this cool in Texas, though certainly as quiet and star-filled, especially at places like Enchanted Rock. And they don't make girls like Naomi, either.

It's unexpected and downright relieving to be around a woman more interested in pictures of baby goats than my rodeo career or my financials. In fact, Naomi gives me the impression she couldn't care less.

When my rodeo career ended, I had a bad reputation for trouble. Fighting, womanizing, driving under the influence. I was headed down a one-way street toward major trouble. But being laid up in the hospital with a broken back gave me plenty of time to reflect on my idiocy and turn my life around with a hefty dose of inspiration from God and the Bible.

My hell-raising days are long gone. I'm ready for a real relationship, the kind that could stand the test of time, and Naomi's the first woman I've met since all this reflecting and changing who fits the bill. But how do I go about forging something strong and enduring with her, or any woman for that matter, when I don't know the first thing about healthy relationships, *and* my work forbids it? Only by the grace of God.

Clearing my throat, I ask, "How much longer are you staying in town, Naomi? Can I talk you into dinner and drinks tomorrow night?"

"No, thank you," she says in gentle, though firm, tones.

"No?" I ask, instantly deflated.

She giggles. "There'll be no cowboy trouble for me. Besides, I'm flying out tomorrow. Have to get back to the hunt for a new salon where I can cut little kids' hair."

That's right. She did mention cutting children's hair as her job. She must have the patience of Job. "I'll hand it to you, Okie. You stick to your guns when it comes to cowboys."

She giggles again, completely disarming me despite the

sting of rejection. "Fool me one, shame on you. Fool me twice—"

"Nah, Okie, you're not the kind of girl who gets fooled twice."

She laughs.

"So, I'm just like all the other guys, then?" I ask, my voice sounding more exasperated than I mean it to.

"Yes," she confirms without hesitation. Arching her eyebrow, she adds, "The same way I'm just like all the other girls."

"No way, Okie. You're one of a kind."

"Okay," she says with a giggle like auditory honey. "Are you ready to fall in love?"

I swallow loudly, shifting the way I'm sitting and making the situation more awkward than it needs to be. I'd love to think she doesn't notice my body language.

She clarifies, "I mean, fall in love with goats?"

I shrug. "Dunno. When it comes to four-legged critters, if I can't ride or eat them, I'm usually not interested."

She shoots a disapproving look at me as if I've stated a sacrilege.

I lean forward, trying to act a little more engaged. "I'm joking. After that buildup, I have to see a baby goat."

She smiles victoriously. "Alright, you've been warned." Naomi hands me her phone in a floral lavender case that is the visual embodiment of her fragrance—lilacs, vanilla, and honey.

I flip through a series of images that could make even the Grinch coo in adoration. Black, white, and fuzzy, they've got impossibly tiny cloven hooves, huge inquisitive eyes, and disproportionately large ears. I can't help but chuckle.

"Well?" she asks, drawing a little closer to me.

I furrow my brows, feigning deep thought when really all I can think about are her stolen glances, flushed cheeks, and the way she bites her lush bottom lip. I inch closer, savoring the heady smell of her floral perfume. My arms ache to hold her, my lips to cover her face in feather-light kisses.

Carefully handing the phone back to her to avoid further touching because my body's already skittering toward overload, I clench my jaw, looking to the side. "You're right. They're pretty darn adorable but not my thing."

"Not your thing?" she repeats, sounding mystified.

I shrug. It's one of the only points of contention between us all week. Otherwise, we're very like-minded. At least based on our text exchanges.

"Okay, what do you have against goats?"

It's a question I'd rather not answer, but I can tell by the look on the blonde's heart-shaped face she's not about to let it go. "My grandparents had billy goats, and they were ornerier than our roosters. Always head-butting the heck out of me when they got the chance." The look in her eyes tells me she's only partially satisfied by my answer.

I don't feel like diving into the rest, though. Like the time Dad beat me to a pulp, resulting in a broken arm and a concussion, because I didn't mind the goat herd properly, and they wreaked havoc on the vegetable garden. It still puts cold shivers down my spine and a nauseous tightening in my throat.

"Whoa, what's the dark look for?" she asks, concern etched on her face.

"Nothing," I answer gruffly.

"Sorry. I didn't mean to bring up bad memories."

I inhale slowly, certain she somehow gets me despite my lack of elaboration. But then, this conversation only confirms what I've noticed while texting and working with her throughout the week. We finish each other's sentences, have a surprising number of shared interests, and appreciate each other's sense of humor. Sometimes, she even has the uncanny ability to read my mind, something I'm not sure how I feel about, considering the scandalous thoughts about the gorgeous Okie filling my head.

"They are cute, though," I say by way of a concession, and her face softens, the concern thankfully fading. The last thing I need is her or anyone else worrying about me. I've always done perfectly fine going it alone. In fact, dealing with people has always caused me trouble. Needing to change the subject and put some fresh distance between myself and painful memories, I smile, ordering, "Look up."

Naomi does, her jaw instantly dropping and her face radiating wonder. "Wow!" she exclaims.

While her eyes absorb the sky, my eyes unrepentantly soak her up, admiring her slim figure shown off to perfection in her red, sleeveless, off-the-shoulder bridesmaid gown. My fingers itch to touch her long, buttery gold curls, and I'd give a whole month's paycheck for a chance to trace kisses along her delicate jawline, finishing at the flirtatious cleft chin that brings her heart-shaped face to a lovely finish.

The moment her eyes drop from the heavens to me, I look away, running my hands through my hair.

"Do you know any of the constellations?"

"Enough to get by while cowboying. You know, the North Star, the Big and Little Dippers, and the like. But you'd need to ask your friend's new husband about the rest. Did you see that spread inside about how he discovered a star and named it after her?"

She smiles, making my insides feel warm and cozy. "Yes, I know all about that. They have the sweetest love story."

"They got lucky for sure," I agree. "Which isn't the case for most people."

To my relief, Naomi nods in agreement. It makes me think she's single even though I can't explain why this should matter to me. But it does ... enough for me to get confirmation straight from the horse's mouth. "And where's your significant other? Couldn't get a week off from work?"

"I don't have one."

Never have I welcomed four words more, and yet I don't understand why. If there's one thing I'm not about to do, it's jeopardize my new position by getting tangled up in relationship drama. The choice has got my guts tied in knots.

"How about you, cowboy?"

I shrug. "Never been much good at all of that."

She chuckles. "Mama always reminds me you only have to be good at it once to be happy. Still, it seems downright impossible sometimes."

I nod toward the house. "Until you see a couple like Luna and Ledger, and it gets you wanting unreasonable things again."

"Is it so unreasonable?"

"That's the million-dollar question," I say, noticing the goosebumps prickling up on Naomi's arms. I remove my dress coat, offering it to her. She shakes her head. But I refuse her refusal until the stubborn beauty finally accepts, happily wrapping my coat around her shoulders. "I reckon for a woman like you, it's absolutely reasonable."

She chuckles, raising her eyebrows. "And what does that mean exactly?"

"I'll spare you the specifics, but you've obviously got everything going for you."

"Maybe." She smirks. "But I've got one mighty thing against me."

Although it shouldn't matter to me, I absolutely need elaboration on what she means. "And what is that one mighty thing?"

"Gravitating towards the wrong kind of men."

How she looks at me now, her face attentive and soft, her lips slightly parted, and her nostrils flaring, tells me everything I need to know about the wrong men. Namely, me.

"And why do you think that is?" I ask, working hard to stay nonchalant, although every part of me needs an answer.

"Let's just say I've kissed a handful of frogs without ever finding a prince."

"Frogs or cowboys?" I ask with a mischievous grin.

"There have been a few cowboys in the frog pond."

I furrow my brows, angry at the thought of another man with her. *What in the heck is wrong with me?* "Makes sense with your dad watching rodeo and you a Sooner."

She nods.

"Back to the whole wrong guys thing. Do you have daddy issues? Or what do you think has caused your romantic dilemma?"

"No daddy issues. I have the best father in the world, although he was often gone growing up because of his job."

"What did he do?" I ask.

"He was a long-distance trucker."

"Sounds like abandonment issues to me. Maybe?" I ask.

"More like they don't make men like they used to," she replies, her Okie accent thick as a slab of homemade butter.

"And how do you wish they made men these days?" I challenge, narrowing my gaze.

"Steady, strong, honest. I'm really not asking for much."

"Maybe you're asking for more than you realize," I counter. "After all, what do you bring to the mix?"

Naomi looks taken aback by the question. "Heart, comfort, loyalty."

I laugh, shaking my head. "Never found that in any girl I dated. Are you trying to tell me you're different from the rest?"

"I'm not trying to tell *you* anything. But I am attempting

to answer your question to the best of my ability. The way you talk, you've dated every woman on the planet."

"I've dated enough ..." I say, looking down at the spot on the ground that I kick with the toe of my boot to distract myself. "I used to be a ramblin' man. Plain and simple."

"And I'm sure you had your pick of the buckle bunnies in your PRCA days."

"You could say that," I concede. "Which goes to show you how ill-equipped I am to make anything last with a woman. Unlike you, who I'm sure will find your match soon enough." My heart sinks a little at the last words, though I'm thoroughly convinced of their import.

"And why do you think you're so ill-equipped?"

I eye her cautiously, shaking my head. "I came out here to make friendly conversation, not get my head examined."

"It's only fair you answer a few of my questions, seeing as you asked about my daddy issues."

I shove my hands in my dress pants pockets, quirking my mouth. She has an obvious point. "It's complicated. I had a rough childhood. A real rough one, and it left its internal scars for sure. The kind no amount of time or love will ever heal."

"Seems odd."

"What does?"

"Giving up on yourself like that. After all, *you* are the only person you can ultimately count on."

"Nope," I reply firmly. "Months in the hospital with rodeo injuries showed me the only person I can count on is my Lord and Savior, Jesus Christ."

"So you *are* a believer?" the blonde asks with a smile so sweet my heart skips a beat.

"Yes, ma'am. In spite of my past."

"Or maybe because of it?"

"Could be," I reply. "Too bad you're not staying longer

and inclined to accept my dinner offer. I could tell you more about it."

She shrugs. "It's probably better this way. After all, it's tough to compete with knitting and baby goats?"

"Would I be competing?" I arch my eyebrow.

"You have a point. Only the right man would be competing."

With a wink, I correct, "You mean the right cowboy?"

Her beet-red cheeks give me the only answer I need.

Chapter Three

NASH

"Wahhhhhhhhhhhhhhh..."

I awaken with a start in the darkened ranch bunkhouse, my ears straining to hear it again. A high-pitched sound. Desperate and forlorn like the cry of a wounded animal or a—

"Wahhhhhhhhhhhhhhhh..."

"What in the heck?" José grumbles, rustling his bedding and making the bunk squeak as he sits up.

Raul's groggy voice joins his. "Is that a baby?"

"Like a human baby?" Dexter chimes in.

"Sounds like it," Lyle concludes.

As soon as the last three words leave Lyle's mouth, the bunkhouse breaks into a chaos of dressing and boot-grabbing before the front door swings wide, and the obnoxious squealing intensifies.

"Dios mío," Raul exclaims. "It *is* a baby!"

A baby? Like heck, it is. This must be a bad dream. I roll over, covering my head with a blanket. I had trouble falling asleep last night after saying goodbye to the lovely blonde

Okie, who I'm pretty sure is taking my heart with her. But what can I do about it?

The spunky woman couldn't have made it any clearer that she wants nothing to do with me. Or cowboys in general. I suppose I can't blame her, seeing as most of us would rather ride off alone in the sunset than commit to the responsibilities of domesticity.

"Wahhhhhhhhhhhhhhhh..."

The guys must've let whatever's making that noise into the bunkhouse because now it's at least five times louder. The sound slices through the quiet of the pre-dawn air, splitting my head and inspiring me to jam my fingers into my ears.

If Randall were here instead of on some ghost town camping trip with his dream girl and her son, he would never let things get this out of hand this early.

"What does it say?" Dexter hollers over the high-pitched banshee noises.

Paper crackles, and then Keaton chuckles deep in his throat. "Looks like somebody just babied themselves out of a job."

"Nash Carter, front and center."

My stomach drops. I can't pretend I didn't hear that. Stiffly, I sit up on my cot, squinting into the bright lights of the room. "Can't a man get a good night's sleep around here?"

"Not with your baby wailing, Carter," Dexter declares, raising his eyebrow.

"My what?"

On the dining table the men stand around in the kitchen, a baby car seat holds a red-faced, screaming bundle swaddled in pale blue blankets. I stare at the menace, going through a mental rundown of who, how, and when this might be possible. Although I'm not ruling it out, the chances are slim.

"Your baby. You have a hearing problem, Carter?"

I open my mouth to answer, but Keaton cuts me off. "Sure must because I specifically heard Eldon warn everyone not to bring any drama around, especially of the female persuasion."

Jumping to my feet, I cross the distance to Keaton, who holds a piece of folded binder paper. Snatching it from him and glaring at the baby, who continues to scream like a fire alarm, I immediately recognize my older sister's messy handwriting. I shake my head, my heart sinking.

"This is from my sister, Nell," I explain, running a hand through my hair and pacing back and forth to the rhythm of the baby's cries. Anger seizes me. It wouldn't be the first time my family's shown up in some way to mess up my life. No matter how hard I work to get out from under their irresponsible mess, they always drag me back in. But this takes the cake.

The gears in my head start turning, and I explain, "This is my sister's handwriting, and it says he's my nephew, Ambrose."

The ranch hands look at me unblinking, and I realize not only am I repeating myself but they've already read the note. I'm still far from processing the whole situation, though, which makes stating the obvious necessary.

"Why would she do this?" I mutter under my breath, pacing back and forth like a man obsessed with the answerless question.

"Did anyone see or hear a car pull up?"

They shake their heads. Keaton, a dark-haired cowboy with a long beard and a predominant widow's peak, scrubs his eyes with the heels of his hands, and Dexter jumps up, heading for the coffee machine. The uncontrolled crying of the boy in the seat makes it clear there will be no more shut-eye tonight.

I race to the door, peering out into the blackness. But to no avail. Whoever left the baby is long gone. The early morning air feels refreshing, and every step away from the screaming is a welcome one. But I can't stand out here forever, especially since Ambrose is my responsibility, at least temporarily. So, I return to the stuffy bunkhouse with its desperate wailing.

Raul asks, scrunching his forehead, "Aren't you going to go after her?"

I shrug, knowing my sister too well. "She abandoned her own flesh and blood. She doesn't deserve a second chance to hurt him. Besides, I've got better ways to track her down than chasing her across the ranch."

One call to my grandparents will do far more than trying to talk sense into Nell. She still relies on them for regular financial help, which means they have a leverage over her that I never will. Opening old wounds and rehashing family relationships better left behind fills me with a nauseous apprehension, though.

The other ranch hands eye me uncomfortably.

José's attention turns ambivalently to the little guy, before peering into a pale blue bag next to him. "Diapers, formula, bottles, pacifiers," he narrates with a tinge of a Chihuahuan accent. Victoriously pulling out a pacifier, he sticks it in the baby's mouth, and the auditory assault stops.

"Thank goodness!" Lyle exclaims, running his hands through his salt-and-pepper hair before tugging on his beard.

"Thank you," I repeat, looking at José as if his face somehow contains the answers I'm looking for. *What do I do? Where do I start?* Child protective services will want to start a case, I imagine, which requires documentation. Documentation starts where this all began, with the wailing on the porch.

"Who saw him first?" I ask, looking from face to face.

Raul steps forward. "I did."

"Okay, we need to put Ambrose back outside right where

you found him, so I can take pictures to document this for CPS."

He nods.

"What in the world was Nell thinking?" I say out loud to the gathered ranch hands. "This place is crawling with coyotes, wolves, mountain lions, badgers, and bears. It's lucky he's still alive."

The men nod somberly as gruesome visions of what could have happened fill my head. "Did anyone hear any knocking or anything before the crying started?"

They shake their heads. My stomach roils as I wonder how long Ambrose sat out there before the crying began.

Crossing the distance to the baby car seat, which includes a large handle for carrying, I pick it up, leading the little guy back outside. "Raul, can you show me where he was when you found him?"

"Right over here," he says, helping me position him carefully. "And there was a blanket over the front of him."

I shiver in the pre-dawn chill, horrified by my sister's choices. CPS has to know what she did. How she endangered her child's life without a second thought. As I snap photos, my mind races. All it would have taken is one predator and the ranch hands sleeping a little harder for tragedy.

I'm spitting mad at Nell, and there's nothing I can do about it as I head back inside, plopping the seat back on top of the table.

"Your sister's some mother." Keaton scowls.

I nod, crossing my arms. "I told y'all when I first started working here. I'm not proud of my past or my family. But I'm committed to securing a better future."

Dexter shakes his head, disbelief written on his face. "Wait, does that mean she drove all the way up from Texas to drop this little guy off?"

I shrug. "She's all over. Haven't kept track of her in years.

The real question is how she found out I'm working here?" My mind races as I look down at the toes of my cowboy boots. "She must've gotten it out of my grandparents." Nobody else in my family knows about my new employment. I've kept it this way purposely to make sure none of them can pull stunts like this.

"Whatever the case," Dexter chimes in, handing me a cup of strong black coffee. "He can't stay here. Eldon'll be madder than a kicked hornet's nest if he gets wind of this."

My stomach twists. I'm a cowboy at the end of my rope in more ways than one. Since injuries took me off the circuit, I've felt aimless, directionless. Getting the job at Heart's Desire Ranch has been the best luck I've had in ages, and I don't want it to end before it really begins. In fact, I hope to leverage this position into my own place someday, as I told Naomi last night.

"The only sensible thing to do is turn him into CPS," I say, blowing on my hot coffee carefully before taking a sip. "I'll make an appointment as soon as they'll see me."

The ranch hands look somber as they nod in a line, staring at me.

Dexter adds, waggling his eyebrows, "I hope this isn't the beginning of more trouble out of you, Nash."

"Nah, it won't be," I promise.

"Ahh," Raul says, admiring the baby with his flushed cheeks and tranquil expression. "He may be a loud little sucker, but he's also a cute one."

"Yeah," I agree uneasily. "Hopefully, CPS can get him into a good home with people who'll take decent care of him." My mind wanders back to moments from my own childhood, and a shiver runs the length of my spine. I know better than anyone what it's like to be an unwanted child. So does Nell, which makes her act all the more unforgivable.

"Fortunately, there's not much going on today apart from

cleaning up after the wedding," Dexter says. "So, there's no better day for calling in sick. Just don't make a habit of this."

"A habit of this?" I ask, exasperation finally getting the better of me.

José claps a hand on my shoulder, reassuring me, "It's okay, man. You'll get this sorted out, and everything will be cool."

"I sure hope so," I say, feeling angrier by the minute as denial of the situation gives way to resignation. "Leave it to my family to try to mess up my life yet again."

Lyle frowns. "I feel you on that one, man. You're not the only one running away from a less-than-enviable past."

Raul counters, "But the little guy is family. Can't you find some buckle bunny from your rodeoing days to help you with him? Maybe you could stay in the cabin we just spiffed up?"

Raul refers to a small cabin on the southern end of the property that was used by a former ranch hand and his family until recently.

I shake my head. "I couldn't ask Eldon or Chase for a favor like that."

"Yes, you could," Raul replies, stony-faced. "This ranch always puts family first."

Before any more speculating can happen, I cut it off at the root. "No need for that. Ambrose doesn't belong with me anyway. CPS will take him, and I'll get back to work. End of story. My apologies, though, for this less-than-optimal start to a Monday."

The bunkhouse door swings open, and Eldon comes in all business, stroking his prominent salt-and-pepper handlebar mustache. "Y'all are up—" he pauses mid-sentence, staring at the baby in the carrier on the table. "What in the world?" The old man eyes the ranch hands quizzically as my stomach sinks into the ground. Here it is. The beginning and end of my new job.

"It's Nash's," Lyle chimes in before the question gets asked.

"Nash's?" Eldon's furry eyebrows hit the ceiling as he looks in my direction, his face swirling with curiosity and sternness.

I clear my throat, stepping forward. "Yes, sir. Actually, he's my sister's baby. There was a note pinned to him when we found him this morning on the bunkhouse steps."

"But how could anybody get on the property with the gates closed?"

"Sir," Dexter reminds. "We left the gate open for the wedding guests who trickled out late into the night.

The ranch foreman shakes his head. Narrowing his eyes at me, he asks, "And what are you planning on doing with him?"

I shrug. "I guess take him to CPS. Not sure what else I can do."

"Well, you could keep him."

"No, sir." I chuckle.

He scrutinizes my face. "Family's family, as far as I'm concerned."

"But I need my job on the ranch."

"You could take the family cabin we cleaned out a few days ago."

I grimace. "But I couldn't bring him out cowboying with me during the day."

Eldon quirks his mouth. "Yeah, and he'd be more than a handful for Véronique. You could finally settle down with a woman."

The whole bunkhouse roars at that unlikely pronouncement.

"Or you could hire a nanny, maybe?"

"A nanny?" My head spins at the suggestion. And it puts a pretty little Okie blonde back on my mind. After all, Naomi cuts kids' hair. How different can nannying be? And it would allow me the chance to get to know her better and maybe keep her from leaving me. After all, she admitted she wants to live in Ouray near her best friend, Luna.

Still, the whole thing's far-fetched. Gruffly, I say, "If you're okay with me taking the day off, I'll drive the baby into Montrose, where I can consult with CPS about next steps. I may be family, but there have to be better options for him."

Chapter Four

"You've got to be kidding me," I lament, staring up at the flight information display board at Montrose Regional Airport. My flight to Denver has just been delayed for the third time due to raging thunderstorms. As I approach the counter yet again to talk to airline staff, fury and frustration mix.

But I'm far from the only one. It looks as if the entire flight passenger list has lined up, which nudges me to move faster, falling somewhere in the middle of the gathered ensemble of angry travelers. This is going to take a while. But I don't really have anywhere else to be.

A crackling boom of thunder pierces the atmosphere of the terminal. I shiver as my eyes strain towards the vast wall of windows, looking out on dark, angry storm clouds. Lightning flickers menacingly ... so close I wonder if it hits one of the airport's lightning rods. Colorado spares no expense or effect when it comes to afternoon thunderstorms.

Fortunately, my bestie and her new husband, Ledger, don't have to worry about airlines. They're road-tripping to

Rocky Mountain National Park for their honeymoon. As I stand in line waiting, I look up rental cars, too, weighing my options for driving back to California.

I'm currently between salon jobs and recently completed a summer internship with Monterey Bay Aquarium. So, a delay of a few days won't be devastating. But it will be highly annoying in terms of the little things like canceling upcoming spa days, dates with new guys, and outings with friends. My head spins as I make a list in the text app on my phone.

By the time I reach the front of the line, the list feels intimidating, and I'm in no mood for squabbling. Mama's voice fills my head as I force a smile. "You attract more flies with honey than vinegar." Still, the anger lurking beneath the smile feels hot and dangerous. As if any answer apart from "Your plane is leaving in five minutes" could set it off.

"Hi," I say with a fake smile. "I'm on delayed flight 1678, which means I'm going to miss my connecting flight to Los Angeles from Denver. Do you have any workarounds for travelers like me?"

"Short of calling in a favor to the weather gods? Not so much. But the airline is offering free drink vouchers to the bar." The immaculately groomed black flight attendant with glittery lavender eye shadow and hot pink lipstick nods towards the bar a short distance down the terminal.

"No offense, but I'm not here for a drink. I need to get home. What are my best options at this point?"

"I understand your frustration. Every person in line before you voiced similar complaints. Let me assure you we're working on getting everyone re-routed ... *eventually*. Your name has been added to the waitlist, and we will keep you updated as we know more. My sincere apologies for this inconvenience."

I exhale slowly, massaging my fingers into my temple. "Are

you able to give me an ETA or guesstimate on when I may get to fly out? Or should I prepare to spend the night?"

The flight attendant clicks rapidly on the computer keyboard in front of her, then scrolls down with the mouse. Her eyes dart back and forth, and she purses her lips, knitting her brows. "For your particular destination, we only fly out of this airport once a day. If you could get to Denver, though, your options would open up."

"*Can* you get me to Denver?" I ask, feeling like this question is so obvious I shouldn't have to voice it.

"In a couple of days."

"In a couple of days?" My eyebrows launch into my hairline.

"Yes, ma'am. We're a small airline, and most of our flights leave in the afternoon. If the weather forecast is correct, you're bound to be here for a few days." She leans closer, absorbing the anger in my gaze. "I'm not supposed to tell you this, but I'd rent a room if I were you. Before everyone else decides to follow suit."

I scowl. "That's great."

"Sorry to be the bearer of bad news. But this is a beautiful part of Colorado. Might as well make the most of your time here."

"So, what do I do about my checked baggage?"

"It will be available at Baggage Claim within the hour, and make sure you have our app. That and email are where you'll receive updates to your itinerary."

"There's really no other way?"

"I'm so sorry, ma'am. But barring an act of God, I'd get comfortable."

I shake my head, walking resignedly away from the counter as the attendant waves up the next group of disgruntled passengers. As annoyed as I am by this development, I have to count my blessings. Things could always be worse.

Like having to be the poor woman relaying this information to a huge line of seething individuals.

I plop down in the first empty seat I see, my purple rolling carry-on poised in front of me as I start searching for nearby hotel rooms. I don't have the money budgeted for this. I'm already using up my rainy day savings to stretch resources until I locate a new salon to work out of. *This* is the last thing I need.

Suddenly, Nash's number lights up my phone. My heart jumps into my throat as I strain to answer without sounding breathy. "Hello?"

"You answered? I thought you'd be in the air right about now."

"It's a long story... Is everything okay?" I can't for the life of me think of why the handsome, rootless cowboy would call me.

"Yes—"

"Wait, is that a baby crying in the background?" The sound is as unmistakable as it is unexpected.

"Yes," he says in low tones, like he doesn't want other people to hear his conversation.

"You really are a ramblin' man, then—" A baby's wailing cuts off the rest of my sentence.

"No, the baby isn't mine, although it might as well be."

"What does that mean?" I knit my brows.

"His name's Ambrose, and he's my nephew. It's a long, sad story that you don't want to hear. But anyhow, this morning, he turned up on the front step of the ranch's bunkhouse screaming at the top of his lungs, and I haven't been able to get him to calm down. You were the first person I thought of, what with your children's hairdressing skills and being from a big family and all. What would you do in my situation to make the crying stop?"

My head spins at his explanation. "Turned up? How does

a baby turn up at a ranch? You mean, your sister left him with you for babysitting or something?"

He exhales sharply, muttering, "More like abandoned him."

"Oh my goodness."

"Yeah, like I said, long, sad story that you don't want to know about. But I have two hours to kill before my appointment with Child Protective Services, so I wanted to get your advice on what to do."

Of all the men to be in this situation, Nash has got to be the most ironic. No amount of cowboying or rodeoing could prepare him for this.

I reply, baffled, "And I was the first person you thought to call?"

"Yes," he says hesitantly. "You've been the level-headed problem-solver every step of the way for Luna's wedding. Figure you'd know what to do now."

"Well, thank you, Nash," I say. "First off, how old is Ambrose?"

I hear him counting under his breath before he answers, "Round about six months old."

"Okay, and you said he showed up at the bunkhouse this morning. Did your sister leave any diapers, formula, or pacifiers?"

"Yes, and the pacifier worked for a good while. But then, he started bawling again and won't stop no matter what I do."

"And you've fed him and changed his diaper?"

Nash mutters, "Yes. He drank a whole bottle, and I changed him a few minutes ago. Even figured out how to burp him."

"Have you tried holding him?"

"Holding him?" Nash questions as if I've just asked him whether or not aliens are real.

"Yes, hold him. Maybe he needs to be rocked."

"But the kid's a spitting machine. I don't want that gunk all over my shirt."

"Shirts wash," I scold gently. "And babies need love. Pick up Ambrose and see how he responds."

I hear rustling in the background as the baby continues sobbing. Nash's voice goes tender and whispery. I can't make out what he's saying, but the tone and timbre melt my heart. It's a side of the rugged cowboy I've never heard before.

Suddenly, the call ends. I stare at my phone blankly for a moment. Either my advice worked, or Nash hung up out of anger because it was so ineffective. Either way, the cowboy's well out of his element. Suddenly, a text pops up in the thread we've shared all week:

NASH

> Sorry about that. I figured I'd text now that I've gotten the little guy quieted down a bit

NAOMI

> So, it worked?

> Sure did. See, I knew you were the person to call. But I'm afraid he's going to fall asleep on my chest. What do I do?

I laugh, shaking my head. Talk about inept in the family department.

NAOMI

> Up to you, but I'd probably let him sleep

NASH

> Geez this feels weird

> What? Taking care of your nephew?

> Holding a baby. I can't remember the last time I did this

> Cowboy, I doubt that. You're just more used to the four-legged variety. Pretend he's an orphaned calf or foal

> Point taken

> You'll do fine until CPS can take over

> Yeah...

> What are the ... for?

> Dunno. I have an uneasy feeling about everything

> About the baby or about CPS?

> Ambrose is a pain in the keister, don't get me wrong. But he also did nothing to deserve this. My sister's a first-rate moron, like most of my family. I hate seeing an innocent kid get dragged into the drama

> Yeah, that's rough. Is he asleep yet? Call me back if you'd like to talk in person

> ...

I watch the three dots on my phone for what feels like forever. To the point where I assume Nash must be texting other people. I'm about to lock the screen when another message comes through.

NASH

> Thank you, but I've already bothered you enough. Good luck with your flight

NAOMI

I'm going to need it

Why?

The airline's telling me another connecting
flight to Denver is probably a few days
away at the earliest because of the weather.
So that means either renting a car to
Denver and trying to beg, steal, and borrow
a brand new flight or staying in Montrose

Why don't you come back to Ouray?

To do what?

I don't know, but it's got to be a whole lot
prettier than Montrose

You have a point, but I'll figure it out

You sure? I'm headed that way with
Ambrose. I could pick you up afterward and
bring you back to the ranch

And then what?

There's an open cabin on the south end of
the property where married ranch hands
typically live. We cleaned it up the other
day, but it's just sitting there. I can't imagine
Chase and Chanel would be opposed to
you staying there for a couple of days

And how would I get there?

Like I already offered. I'm more than happy
to give you a ride

And CPS is in Montrose?

Yes

> Thank you. I'll let you know if I change my mind. Keep me posted on what happens with Ambrose

> Will do

Nash's offer is far more inviting than it should be. And I know my options don't end there. Luna and Ledger would happily let me stay in their cabin while they're honeymooning. But I don't want to bother my bestie with personal drama on her first married vacation.

Googling local hotels, my eyes bug out as I register the prices. I so don't have the budget for this. Especially when I add additional needs like food, transportation to and from a hotel, and unexpected costs more than likely to come up. It's as if The Universe wants to keep me permanently broke. Or maybe Colorado doesn't feel like letting me go. But for what reason?

I could call my parents and beg for money. I know they'd gladly front me, but I'm a twenty-four-year-old woman. I need to figure this out without running back to Mama and Daddy. Moreover, I hate feeling like I owe anyone, even my own flesh and blood, anything.

Making my way downstairs to the Baggage Claim area, I grab my luggage from the carousel, feeling angry enough to scream. I don't have the money for this complication. Maybe I can sleep in the airport tonight? It's one night ... *hopefully*. I can get through this, right?

I could almost make myself a cozy little corner in one of the terminals, using rolled-up clothes for pillows. And I could splurge on one of the cozy blankets from an airport store. It would be far cheaper than the room rates I've researched.

The airport is climate-controlled. It has edible, though expensive, food and my pick of bathrooms. What more do I need?

Safety, security, a bed, and a hot shower.

Staying in the airport sounds like the makings of a miserable night. And if one day drags into two or more? I'd do better to rent a car and drive at that point. Or take Nash up on his offer.

Chapter Five

NASH

Sitting in the CPS waiting room, Raul's statement and question from this morning in the bunkhouse play through my head over and over again. Could I find a woman to help me with Ambrose? And is abandoning the boy at CPS really my only option? Or is it another Carter family cop-out that makes me no better than Nell and my parents?

I cross my arms over my chest, staring at the baby. Ambrose, in turn, eyes me raptly from his car seat on the ground, gumming his fist.

"What?" I finally grumble, feeling a bit self-conscious talking to a baby. The round-faced infant with rosy cheeks, a cascade of golden locks, and big, blue eyes absorbs me, narrowing his eyes. I wonder how all of this feels from his point of view.

Around us, families sit. Older kids and teens morosely wait, staring off into space, while younger kids gather around a corner filled with toys. Other kids of all ages sit poised in their chairs, poring over everything from picture books to YA novels. The off-white walls of the facility and pale pink carpets are designed to calm people, I'd wager. And the painfully generic landscapes on the walls could be anywhere and nowhere at the same time.

Outside, thunder cracks loudly, making more than one person jump in their chair. The lights flutter momentarily, and some of the adults look up concerned.

An outage would certainly top off an otherwise highly eventful day. I imagine Naomi feels the same way. Ironically, she's only a few miles away, languishing at the Montrose Regional Airport. I wish I could say our earlier texting conversation had gone better.

Ironically, she's the only woman I've been able to think of who could be a good temporary mom for Ambrose. After all, she did mention being a children's hairdresser. If she can get a small child to sit still while messing with their locks, I imagine a baby would be a piece of cake for her.

And that pretty heart-shaped countenance with that irresistible cleft chin and smooth Okie accent? Well, if I were Ambrose, I know that's the face and voice I'd want to see and hear.

The baby eyes me now, scowling and furrowing his brow as though in deep thought. Is he mirroring my pensive look? I can't help but laugh, sucked up into the cuteness of the tiny guy. "Sorry, buddy. As much as I'd like to get you a hot mama, she's got better things to do than mess with us." *Like sitting alone in an airport terminal...*

Don't even let your mind go there, Nash. She wants nothing to do with you. The internal scolding doesn't change the fact that somewhere deep down in the most authentic part of me, I *would* like something to do with her.

"Mr. Carter?" A male voice draws me out of my reverie, and I look up at a short, tan man with thick, wavy black hair and snapping black eyes. Standing, I grab the handle of the baby car seat and carrier ensemble, reminding myself this is theoretically the last time I should have to carry it or look at this adorable little nephew of mine again. The realization has the opposite of the intended effect, making me strangely nostalgic.

Why? I haven't even spent twenty-four hours with the kid. Logic doesn't help one bit with this odd feeling.

Striding towards the man, I respond, "I'm Nash Carter." I reach out my free hand to shake his.

"And I'm Gregory Watson. Right this way."

He leads me through a maze of hallways into a bleak, gray room without windows and only a couple of chairs and a table. "Have a seat," he urges, and I take my place, setting Ambrose's car seat down next to me.

I swear, all day, this baby's been a wailing, screaming pain in the butt. Now, though, he's pleasant and quiet, as if he's trying to get into my good graces. Too late for that. I'm the last thing this baby needs.

Watson and I go through the motions. I show him the pictures on my phone and explain how everything went down. He takes notes on a laptop as we talk, stopping every now and again to stroke his chin pensively.

"What's the best contact number for your sister?"

"My grandparents are the best way to get a hold of her. Let me get their number for you." I swipe through my contacts until I find what I'm looking for, reading the number to him as he writes.

"Do you understand how guardianship works and what the responsibilities and stipulations are?" Watson eyes me pointedly.

"Guardianship?" I nearly choke on the words.

The man nods, not looking the least bit surprised or amused by my response.

"No, you can't mean me. I'm just a bachelor cowboy. I'm definitely not cut out for babies and the whole fatherhood thing."

Watson shrugs. "Well, you are the nearest of kin geographically speaking. We'll reach out to your parents and other siblings, too, though."

"That's a terrible idea," I spit out before thinking.

Watson raises a questioning eyebrow.

"If you want to turn him into a delinquent and criminal, send him to my parents. If you want him to end up dead, send him back to my sister."

Watson scrunches his face. "I see. Well, the appropriateness of a placement is something the family court must ultimately decide. We can only make recommendations."

"Understood. But my sister left him on the doorstep of the bunkhouse where I work as a ranch hand. There's no telling what predators might have been stalking around there this morning."

Watson scowls. "Yes, you already showed me pictures. That said, sir, once you sign away guardianship rights, you won't have any say in your nephew's welfare."

I shift uneasily in my seat, feeling the ancient weight of being an unwanted child clobber me over the head like a ton of bricks.

"Where a family placement isn't possible, the foster care system is another option. Usually, babies are in high demand, but the state's in desperate need of foster parents at the moment, so if there's any way you would consider caring for your nephew until we find a suitable placement, it would be greatly appreciated."

I eye the baby, and he smiles at me, blabbering and trying to blow me raspberries. I may not be into all of this kid stuff, but I can't deny how adorable the little guy is.

"If you would like to sign over guardianship, we can get that paperwork going—"

Unthinking and unfiltered, I surprise myself, interrupting,

"Can I get a minute or two to think this through? I need to reach out to somebody."

Watson's eyebrows jump into his hairline as he shrugs. "Yeah, sure. Let me go get the necessary paperwork for you to fill out." He stands unceremoniously, striding from the room.

What in the heck are you doing, Nash? You can't possibly be contemplating keeping this baby. You're the last person on the planet who should raise a child. Well, maybe the last person after your idiot sister.

I stare down at Ambrose, and he coos, laughing and flashing a big toothless grin in my direction. Darn, he's adorable. Even more adorable than the baby goats Naomi insisted on showing me last night. *And he resembles me as a baby.* I shake my head, a dangerous plan forming in my mind.

For the millionth time, my heart nudges me. *Ask Naomi for help. Or better yet, hire her as a nanny.*

My phone buzzes, and I pull it out of my pocket. Smiling broadly, I read:

NAOMI

If you're still in Montrose and okay with the whole picking me up at the airport thing, I would greatly appreciate it

NASH

Only if I can talk you into staying for longer than a few days

What do you mean?

I have a job proposition for you

Uh-oh...

Don't sound so excited. If I decided to keep my nephew, would you consider being his nanny?

A nanny? I'm a children's hairdresser not a nanny

I'm going to cut to the chase, Sparky

Sparky?

Yes, because that Okie tongue of yours is always spitting and sparking fire

Wow, is that your idea of a compliment?

You and I both know you're not sitting around waiting on compliments from me

True, Tex. But back to your question... Becoming Ambrose's nanny would mean moving to Ouray

It would. At least until I can figure out my next move

I thought you had already ... taking him to CPS

I can't give him up

But you can't keep him either

I could with your help

You're funny

To the contrary, I need you, Naomi

...

I stare intently at the three dots, holding my breath. If I've come on too strong, it's all over for Ambrose. One thing I know for certain is I can't do this alone.

But if Naomi would relent and give me a chance, I could

prove to her there's more to me than bad-boy cowboy stereo-types. When I can't wait another minute. I text back:

> You said it yourself the other night. You have no job to go home to. California's too expensive, and you'd like a change of pace. I can offer you that

NAOMI

> What happened to the lifelong bachelor cowboy I danced with last night?

> Nothing's happened to me. But I'm also a man who knows when he needs to do right. And everything about this situation tells me I need to do better for my nephew at least until CPS can find a permanent placement for him

> Okay

> Okay what?

> Okay, I'll be Ambrose's nanny. At least until I figure out my next job or Ambrose finds a permanent placement

> Wow. Thank you

I swallow hard to clear the lump forming in my throat. I don't know why Naomi's agreement to watch Ambrose hits me so hard, but it does. I clench my jaw, feeling downright emotional because Naomi's exactly the kind of woman I needed when I was a kid. Level-headed, strong, compassionate, reliable.

NAOMI

> Text me when you get to the airport?

NASH

Yes. Which terminal?

C

Bye

Goodbye

I stare down at Ambrose, my face and voice grave as I say, "What in the world am I thinking? I'm the last man on earth cut out to raise a baby." His countenance scrunches again, and I'm certain that's the game now, mimicking my facial expressions.

The next call makes my chest hurt like I have heartburn, but I have to make it. Besides, Eldon was the first to suggest it. The phone rings a couple of times before the ranch foreman picks up. "Hello."

"Eldon, it's Carter."

"Carter, is it done?"

"Yes," I reply, looking for the right words. "But done differently than I originally intended. Does the offer still stand to take over the cabin? If so, I've got a nephew and a new nanny to bring back to Heart's Desire."

"Shoot, this is going to take some getting used to. You're the last man on the planet I could ever imagine as a single dad. But I think you've made the honorable decision under the circumstances."

"We'll see about that," I say, removing my cowboy hat and swiping the back of my hand across my forehead.

"I'm going to go pick up my new nanny, and then we'll head in your direction."

"So, the nanny will be staying with you?" Eldon asks.

I shrug even though I know he can't see it. I haven't thought that far ahead. "I guess so. Isn't that how that kind of thing works?"

"Need I remind you there's only one adult-sized bed in the place? The rest are children's bunk beds."

I shake my head, still trying to wrap my head around what I'm doing. Sleeping arrangements are the least of my concerns. "I can take the couch or the floor."

"Okay. It'll be ready when you get back. But I'd suggest stopping for groceries in Montrose since you won't be eating in the bunkhouse from now on."

I scowl, shaking my head. I also hadn't thought that through. This arrangement is starting to sound downright domestic. I hope Naomi'll be happy to see a grocery store after spending the day in an airport. Speaking of airports and her current situation, I notice I haven't heard thunder in a little while.

As Watson enters the room again carrying paperwork, I ask, "Has the storm let up?"

"Seems to have." He plops a pile of papers in front of me with a pen. "Here's what you need to fill out to surrender guardianship."

Shaking my head, I level my gaze on him. "Actually, I've changed my mind. What do I need to sign to keep Ambrose as a foster placement? At least until a more permanent home can be located."

"Oh good," Watson says on a long exhale. "We'll need to expedite a background check and ensure there are no safety issues."

"Whatever you need."

Chapter Six

NAOMI

I stand outside the airport terminal with my luggage propped next to me, waving when I see Nash's familiar truck. As he pulls up, his face serious, what I've agreed to finally hits me.

Am I really temporarily relocating to Ouray to nanny a bachelor cowboy's baby surprise? Yes, I am, and it sounds like a plot good enough to make a Hallmark movie. But I remind myself as I watch the impossibly handsome man double park before jumping out and grabbing my luggage to throw into the pickup bed that this is no romance movie. He wears a white and blue striped button-down shirt tucked in, Wranglers, and brown work boots. Everything fits to perfection, the epitome of mouthwatering.

No, Naomi, get a hold of yourself. This is a mutually beneficial agreement that'll help out a baby in need. That's it.

My hand rests on the passenger handle of the truck when Nash's deep voice scolds testily, "Don't even think about it." Closing the distance between us in a couple of long strides, he opens the door for me, offering me his hand to boost me into the seat. He hesitates for a moment, and I half expect him to lean into the cab and fasten my seatbelt.

Please don't. Please don't. Although he's unaware of my internal struggle, thankfully, the cowboy thinks twice about overdoing it in the gentleman department, closing the passenger door instead.

I turn, staring at the back of a rear-facing car seat. Next to it sits a powder blue diaper bag. The driver-side door slams shut, and Nash eyes the rearview mirror before pulling out and driving away from the airport. His jade-hued eyes meet mine, and we both grin far larger than we need to.

Nash is the first to wipe the smile off his face, shaking his head and lamenting, "I cannot believe this day. If you'd told me twenty-four hours ago all of this was going to happen... Well, shoot."

"As I recall, less than twenty-four hours ago, you were singing the praises of the single life. So, how does it square with instant fatherhood?"

"That's the million-dollar question, Sparky. And I'm not sure that it does, but I couldn't leave him behind, an unwanted child." He stares straight ahead as he talks, his voice steely. "Besides, they reassured me that normally a baby's easy to place. I can't imagine you'll have to stick around for too long. That is unless you decide to relocate permanently to be closer to Luna."

I chuckle, combing my fingers through my long, blonde hair absentmindedly to soothe my nerves. "After the day I've had, I'm just happy to be anywhere other than an airport terminal. I wasn't looking forward to sleeping there tonight."

"Yeah, that sounds awful."

"Of course, we'll see how it goes with Ambrose tonight," I whisper in soft tones, looking into the backseat again. "Oh, my goodness! He has the cutest, fattest little fingers."

Nash glances back in the rearview mirror, seeing the balled fist I'm staring at.

"It's alright. Not as cute as baby goats, though."

"Infinitely cuter than baby goats," I correct.

"Naomi, it sounds like you have a baby problem."

"Guilty as charged. Is there any way we could stop by a craft store on the way back to the ranch? I want to get some yarn to start knitting the little guy a cap and blanket."

Nash nods. "Yeah, I figured we need to stop for groceries and whatever supplies you think the baby needs."

I cock my head to the side, smiling broadly at the handsome cowboy with the chestnut-colored hair and beard. He returns my gaze warmly, asking, "What does that look mean?"

I shrug. "Just trying to figure out how you're holding up."

"Holding up? How do you mean? Because of Ambrose?"

"Because of all of it. A baby, a woman, heading to the grocery store. You must feel downright domestic."

He removes his Stetson, running a hand through his thick hair. "Don't remind me. Next thing I know, there'll be baby goats and alpacas in the backyard." He winks, and my heart flutters faster than a hummingbird's wings.

"Oh, that's how you'll know you're a goner, then?"

He arches a thick eyebrow, drawling, "Sparky, you and I both know I'm already neck-deep in trouble. Whether or not either of us wants to admit it."

The statement is ambiguous, begging for interpretation in countless ways. So, why does it make me feel all warm and melty inside, like chocolate chip cookies fresh from the oven? Leaning a little closer to the cowboy, I catch the scent of his masculine cologne—all cypress, sandalwood, with a dash of I could-get-used-to-this.

Turning back towards the window and looking out at the streets of Montrose that we pass on the way to the grocery store, I remind myself, *Keep your head on straight, Naomi.*

And don't get attached to this guy. He's one big walking red flag, no matter how handsome he may look or how charming he can act.

A gurgling and cooing draws my eyes to the backseat and the baby, who's apparently awake again and entertaining himself. I haven't even seen the little guy's face yet, and I already know he's going to be trouble, too. I must keep my heart extra guarded to avoid falling for this duo.

Nash parks near the back of the lot, taking up two spaces with his dually. He rushes around the front of the truck to open the door for me, and I have the impression yet again that we're on a date. The way his cheeks darken, and his warm eyes catch mine for a fraction of a second further confirms the feeling. But then he awkwardly backs away, and I remind myself he and I are employer and employee. That's it.

Opening the extended cab door, he motions resignedly for me to have a look at Ambrose. I shuffle around him, leaning into the truck's backseat, gasping. Covering my mouth, I turn, my eyes catching Nash's. "Oh my goodness! This baby's adorable, and he's the spitting image of you..."

I barely have a chance to kick myself for the unintended compliment when the cowboy's voice cuts through the awkward silence, saying, "So, you think I'm adorable?"

I shrug, straightening and giving him a disinterested once-over. "I suppose you were as a baby."

He chuckles, putting his hands on his hips and shifting his weight from one boot to the other. "Enough about me. Show me some of that nanny magic."

"Nanny magic? If that's what you're looking for, I'm not your girl. But I *can* cut Ambrose's hair and keep him clean, well-fed, and loved."

"Sounds like nanny magic to me," Nash says gruffly.

Leaning into the backseat, I reach out a finger to Ambrose, and he reflexively grabs it. Big blue eyes stare up at me, his brows furrowing, and he chuckles, revealing a toothless grin. "Oh my goodness, aren't you just the cutest thing on God's green earth?" I say to the baby.

Behind me, Nash grumbles, "You know, every time you compliment Ambrose, Okie, I'm going to take it, by extension, as a commentary on what you think of my appearance."

Looking over my shoulder, I roll my eyes, catching him admiring my figure from behind. Nash looks down, his angular cheeks glowing. Unfastening Ambrose and pulling him out of the car seat, I marvel at how lightweight and compact the little guy is. He presses a fat baby palm to my cheek, staring at me with large, curious eyes.

I open my mouth to spew first impressions, thankfully catching myself before I say too much. The truth is, I'm already totally enamored with this little guy. It's love at first sight.

Naomi Donovan, nanny. Who would've ever thought it? I know I'll have plenty to tell Luna when she returns from her honeymoon. But now, I've got to focus on making this baby feel loved, comfortable, and safe. I can tell by the guarded way he regards me he's been through a lot. His little face goes from smiling and jovial to dissolving into fear, and he lets out a high-pitched scream.

"For the love of Pete," Nash grumbles. "Just about anything makes this kid cry."

Ambrose's tentative whimpers turns into full-throttled wails, and I direct Nash, "Please grab his diaper bag and hand me a pacifier if that's what you've been using to calm him.

"Yes, it is," he says, digging through the bag's contents and producing a white one for me. Our fingertips brush as he hands it to me, and I feel alive with a strange yearning I've never known before. *No, Naomi, this man is trouble. Cute baby or not.*

Once inside the store, I beeline for the bathroom, noticing

there's a bad odor coming from the diaper Ambrose currently wears. "I'm going to run inside and change him. We'll be one minute."

Nash looks relieved, nodding vigorously. I get the distinct impression he'd rather do anything than diaper the baby. I may be Ambrose's nanny, but the cowboy's going to have to get used to this very necessary part of raising an infant. I remind myself there will be plenty of time for this.

After cleaning up the little guy, I find Nash outside, leaning against a shopping cart and typing into his phone.

"What are you looking at?" I ask, plopping the baby bag down in the cart.

"Making a list of things we need for Ambrose and ourselves."

I shake my head, still trying to wrap my head around the fact I'm grocery shopping with the "cute guy" from the wedding.

"What?" he asks in low tones that make my knees weak.

"There's a lot of *unforeseen* that could have happened today. Sleeping in an airport, catching a flight from another airline, and finally giving in and renting a car to drive home to California. But grocery shopping with you and a baby? No way."

"I know," he straightens, licking his lips and making no effort to hide the way his eyes drop to my mouth. I sigh, my heart racing. "You look good with a baby on your hip, Okie."

"Do I now?" I giggle, my pulse roaring in my temples. "I imagine you do, too," I retort, silently offering him Ambrose.

But the cowboy shrugs. "He's been tied to my hip all day, and I could use a break. He's been doing a number on my back."

We start down the card aisle and move towards the back of the grocery store where they keep dairy and eggs. "Father's

Day is right around the corner. What should Ambrose and I get you?"

He looks down. "Shucks, Sparky, I'm not thinking nearly that far ahead. Besides, Ambrose'll likely have a placement by then. CPS said it wouldn't take long for a baby, that they're highly sought after."

"I don't like how that sounds," I say without thinking. "Like he's an object rather than a person."

Nash stops, eyeing me carefully. "That's exactly how I felt about that statement, too."

"I wonder what all of this is like from Ambrose's point of view," I say, listening to the baby compulsively suck his pacifier.

"I've also been wondering the same thing. Yet again, you're reading my mind."

"Let's see if it works in reverse," I reply saucily, raising my chin in challenge. Pointing at the shopping cart, I say, "I know what the West Coast calls this contraption and a good portion of Oklahoma, to boot. But what do you call it?"

Nash lazily smiles. "Everyone knows it's a buggy."

"My kind of man," I exclaim.

He tips his hat at me. "That's what I've been trying to make you see all week."

A stupid grin captures my face. I amend, "Vocabulary-wise."

"And thoughts-wise," he adds, tapping his pointer finger against his temple and winking again. "And looks-wise, if I really am the spitting image of Ambrose."

"You're not going to let that go, are you?"

"Never."

I can't help but giggle, staring down at Ambrose's moon face and big, round periwinkle eyes. I whisper to the baby in a voice loud enough for Nash to hear, "You and I both know you're the cuter one."

Nash's face darkens, a tenderness in his eyes I've never seen before as his gaze moves from the baby to me. Clearing his throat and swallowing loudly, he says, "I'm alright with Ambrose being my wingman if that's what it takes." My brows knit, and I open my mouth, but before I can reply, he orders, "Alright, Sparky, direct me where to go."

"We need to hit the baby aisle for sure. Ambrose needs more formula, diapers, wipes, baby food, baby powder, baby shampoo and soap, lotion, and all the stuff." My head spins. A grocery store will only cover so much. "Is there a baby store around here, too? Or maybe a Walmart or Target?"

"Yeah, why?"

"Because, in all honesty, we need a crib and a playpen, a high chair, baby spoons. You know, the kind with the soft rubber edges. A sippy cup or two, more bottles, an activity blanket for tummy time, other toys, a mobile, more clothes, a bathtub…"

Nash stops, his jaw hitting the floor.

"What?"

He shakes his head. "That's a lot to invest in a temporary situation."

"Temporary or not, these are necessities," I counter, my voice straining. Maybe I'm more nervous about this whole situation than I care to admit.

"You know, this shopping trip isn't all about the baby. You and I need to shop for ourselves, too. I don't know what you'd like for dinner, but I can grill up some mean steaks."

"And I make these twice-baked potatoes that are to die for. My grandma's recipe."

"Done," Nash declares, his face softening slightly. "I'm going to have to ease into this whole domestic bliss thing a bit. So, tell me what Ambrose absolutely needs, and we'll go from there."

"Absolutely?" I quirk my mouth in thought, letting my

mind wander back to my younger siblings, which included two sets of twins. "A high chair, spoons, plates and sippy cups, bibs, toys, a baby bath, and a playpen that's also a crib. Some may even come with a built-in mobile—"

"I'm cutting you off there, Okie. For your own good and mine, too."

I giggle, appraising the man's nervous face. "Well, we'll still need to visit a Walmart or Target."

"Which one?"

"It doesn't matter."

He raises an eyebrow. "Do both have yarn for your baby projects?"

My face warms surprised that he remembered. "Oh, yes, yarn! I almost forgot. Walmart, in that case."

Looking at his phone, he shakes his head. "Looks like you'll be keeping me out late like last night. You're a bad influence, Sparky."

Chapter Seven

NASH

A trip to the grocery store turns into a two-hundred dollar food bill, followed by a visit to Walmart that climbs into the triple digits. *Triple digits!*

And all for a rugrat, albeit an adorable one, who my delinquent sister never should have burdened me with. Between the supplies, which Naomi assures me are only the bare necessities and the blonde's nannying paycheck, I don't even want to think about what all this will end up costing me. No wonder I've stayed single all these years. This ball and chain stuff is financially disastrous.

Of course, it's not like I don't have the funds to cover this. During my rodeo days, I did well enough to build a decent-sized nest egg. Last thing I want to do is start tapping into it, though. Of course, what's the point of having it if it isn't for an emergency like this?

My mind swirls with angry thoughts. If Nell was here right now, I'd wring her neck. She's got me more than fit to be tied. I retrieve another trip's worth of plastic bags and boxes out of the truck bed, hoofing them inside.

The voice of an angel seizes my ears as I head into the

cabin Chase and Eldon so kindly offered me, and I freeze ... kind of like my heart, listening to the otherworldly strains. Man, can Sparky sing. I would've never guessed it, and that thick Okie accent of hers gets downright smoky like she's come straight out of the Appalachian backcountry. "Naomi, what in the world are you doing?" I half ask, half scold.

She stops, looking up surprised, and I can't help but admire her lithe frame in a white floral sundress with an acid-wash jean jacket and short, tan cowboy boots. Naomi is everything I could ever want in a woman personified.

The moment the cabin falls silent, Ambrose starts fussing and screwing up his face in what I figured out somewhere around six hours into this extended babysitting nightmare is the precursor to ear-splitting cries. "Singing seems to calm Ambrose. Is your sister, Nell, much of a singer?"

I shake my head, laughing. "Now, that's a funny joke. She's got a voice like an angry burro ... 'course I shouldn't talk because mine's little better."

Naomi chuckles, her eyes soft and loving. Years of woman-izing have warped my sense of women. I'm used to lusty stares filled with expectation. But this look is sweet, tender, and unconditional. There's not much I wouldn't sacrifice to see it twice.

"Wahhhhhhhhhhhhhhhh..."

I shake my head. "Please don't let me bother you. Get back to the singing. I'll keep bringing in everything and then get to assembling it."

I glance around the room, my hands on my hips as Naomi hums gently, casting an immediate spell of calm on the little guy. I can't blame him. She has me eating out of her hand, too. Fortunately, she's too busy to notice.

Steeling my expression and grumbling in a faux attempt at unruliness, I add, "This cabin isn't big enough for all of

Ambrose's stuff. It's going to be baby from one end to the other."

Naomi's eyebrows arch, though she keeps her face trained on Ambrose as she says in sing-song tones that captivate him, "What else would it be filled with, Tex?"

I shift my weight. "Stuff that indicates two adults reside in the place."

"Two adults?" Naomi asks, twisting her head in my direction. "But aren't you sleeping in the bunkhouse?"

"No, ma'am," I reply, crossing my arms over my chest. "Is there a problem?"

She blinks a couple of times, quirking her mouth. Ambrose starts crying the moment her attention leaves him. This baby. He's got her wrapped around his fingers. Making overly expressive facial gestures and eyeing him again, she says in goofy tones, "I guess not. But there are only two bedrooms, so where are *you* going to sleep?"

I exhale, chuckling. "Wherever you want me, darling."

"Darling," she spits like it's a curse word. "The couch."

"Done." The rejection of her tone should put me off. Instead, I watch every move she makes raptly.

I ditch my coat and button-down shirt, heading back towards the door for another round of baby gear. At the truck, I heft a heavy box up onto my shoulder, muscles straining beneath my white T-shirt. I feel eyes on me. Glancing up, I catch Naomi admiring me in the entryway to the kitchen. She looks away guiltily.

"Keep your eyes on Ambrose, Sparky. He's much better looking than me ... even though he *is* my spitting image."

"Literally spitting," she says, looking ruefully at Ambrose and shaking her head at his shiny cheeks. He's a drooling barbarian. Not sure what Naomi sees in him.

Once the living room is filled to the gills with bags and boxes, I ask, "Naomi, darling, where would you like me to start putting stuff together so I can take the kid off your hands for a bit while you cook us up something to eat?"

"Nuh-uh, cowboy," she responds with an exasperated laugh. "First of all, I've already told you I don't do the whole 'darling' thing. Second, I distinctly remember you bragging about your grilling skills earlier."

I remove my hat, shoving a hand into my hair to smooth it. "First off, we say 'darling' in Texas the way Valley Girls say 'like,' so as much as it pains you, you'll have to get used to it. Second, I'm more than happy to grill if you feel like putting all of the other food items together alone while watching the ruffian."

The corners of her mouth turn down. I tense my muscles, prepared for her next smart, Okie response. To my utter surprise, she concedes, "You have a point. But does that mean you'll watch Ambrose while I cook?"

I nod, trying not to grin. "Yes, Naomi, that's the idea." A sense of victory washes over me, not so much because she agreed with me for once but because her baby blues bathe me with a newfound appreciation I could hold onto for a lifetime ... if the stubborn Okie would let me.

Where in the heck are these thoughts coming from? Less than twenty-four hours with Ambrose and Naomi, and you're ready to play house?

One look at Naomi, and I have my answer. *Yes, I am.*

"What's wrong?" The blonde asks apprehensively, her eyes drilling into me some more.

"Nothing," I say, trying to speak the truth but failing to find the right words. "Things were just a lot easier before this kid showed up. Right about now, I'd be making my own grub and relaxing with the other ranch hands. I feel like I have to plan out every move to keep this guy safe."

No wonder my sister dumped him on my doorstep. Thankfully, I don't say the last sentence. Heck, I don't even want to acknowledge thinking it, especially after all my nephew's been through. Nevertheless, having a baby around makes me feel oddly claustrophobic. I can't leave him alone for a minute without dire and immediate consequences. If Naomi weren't here to help, I don't know what I'd do.

I expect Naomi to scold me for my last statement. Instead, the beauty smiles softly, understanding washing over her face. "I know exactly what you mean. As much as I pride myself on being good with kids, I enjoy the certainty of knowing when their hair appointment ends."

I nod, looking down at the toes of my cowboy boots. Her empathy makes me feel things I shouldn't. That I'm seen, understood, even cared for. It inspires a yearning to keep this woman for a lifetime, and I'm afraid my too-warm gaze will give me away.

She continues, "What we're doing with Ambrose is constant, though. I know you didn't want to spend so much on baby gear, but it's absolutely necessary so that we can do basic things, like use the bathroom or take a shower, without worrying about his safety."

I furrow my brows, pleased she understands how I'm feeling but concerned she's ready to turn tail and run. "Are you having second thoughts about the nanny position?"

She shrugs. "No more than you're having second thoughts about going from uncle to daddy."

Daddy. I've never thought of myself as one of those before. But something about how the pretty little Okie says it makes me okay with the label.

You can't start doing this, Nash. Watch yourself. I clarify gruffly, "Only until CPS can find a permanent placement. Hopefully, it'll be quick, so you and I can get back to our lives."

She looks down, smiling ambiguously. I could almost swear I perceive a hint of melancholy on her lips.

It accompanies a new pang in my heart I've never felt before. One that tells me this woman is far more dangerous than I first thought. If I'm not careful, I could end up more than helplessly attracted to her. I could end up *needing* her. Not just for Ambrose but *for me*.

Talk about inviting a world of hurt because I don't see how a woman like her could ever be happy with a deeply flawed man like me. That said, why did God put her in my path? I need to place my faith in Providence, wherever it takes me.

"Why so serious?" Naomi asks, scrutinizing my face. The careful way she examines me is uncomfortable. I'm used to one kind of attention from women. Lust. Not caring, thoughtful, genuine concern.

"Just thinking about the best order to tackle all these projects. Seems like we should get his cage ready first, don't you think?"

"Cage?" She chuckles, arching her brows. "You mean his playpen sleeper?" She returns to addressing Ambrose as she speaks, giving me a break from her intuitive gaze.

"Yeah." I shrug. "Whatever y'all call it."

Her sky-blue eyes snap back to mine, and my heart does a full twirl, like a cowboy flying out of a bronc's saddle. *Danger. Naomi is addictive, unadulterated danger.*

"Actually, we could use his high chair first. That way, Ambrose can sit in the kitchen with me while I put away the groceries and get dinner ready."

"What are we eating?" I ask, my stomach lurching at the thought of food.

She chuckles. "Tofu stir-fry sound good?"

"Tofu what?" I'm going to starve to death if that's Naomi's idea of food.

She shakes her head, chuckling. "The look on your face, Tex. I think we'll stick with the steak and twice-baked potatoes if that works for you. Although next time around, there will be no shirking out of your grilling responsibilities."

"Yes, ma'am," I answer with a lopsided grin and wink. Her cheeks heat, and her nostrils flare as her eyes drop subtly to my lips. *Trouble, trouble, trouble.* "Something wrong?" I murmur, letting my eyes return the favor and noticing how perfectly sculpted and pink her lips are. A sweet invitation only made resistible by the fact she's busy with Ambrose.

"Just trying to figure out your interested, not interested signals. Your body language could confound a CIA agent."

The straightforward nature of her words catches me completely off guard, and I blink hard a couple of times. Unable to think of anything to say, I reply firmly, "I could say the same about you. Good thing we're an employer and employee. You know, to keep things clear."

"Good thing," she answers a little wistfully.

"Now, let me see what I can do about rustling up tools to assemble everything," I narrate, turning on my heels and heading for the door. I need a breather from these two and the odd jumble of emotions they excite.

Chapter Eight

NAOMI

Despite my earlier observation about mixed signals, Nash Carter doesn't know when to stop. After putting everything together in a whirlwind of commotion in the living room, he enters the kitchen, holding a bouquet of freshly picked wildflowers in stunning shades of violet, gold, and purple.

"Those are beautiful, Nash," I exclaim.

He has his Stetson off, and he says gently, "They're pasque flowers, golden banner, and mountain iris. I just want to thank you again for stepping in like this with Ambrose. Hearing you sing to him in the kitchen while you got tonight's meal ready. Well, it did something pretty good to my heart. Honestly, I don't know what I'd do without you here, even though I hate admitting things like that."

"I'm happy we could make this work out ... for the time being."

"For the time being," he echoes, his face suddenly wistful. His actions and words confound me, but I try not to read too much into them. Mama's warned me where mixed signals get a woman ... a broken heart, and that's the last thing I need. It's already going to feel bittersweet when Ambrose gets placed in permanent care, and I've only spent a few hours getting to know the good-natured, chubby-faced infant.

Turning away to hide the befuddled look on my face, I search the kitchen cabinets for a vase, coming up empty-handed.

"That Mason jar would do," the cowboy says, coming up behind me to fetch it from over my head. As he easily grabs it, his body draws so close to mine I feel the heat pouring off him and smell his tempting cypress and sandalwood cologne.

The proximity only lasts for an instant, but it reminds me of how good I felt in his arms on the wedding reception dance floor. It also makes me long for more than the confines of our employer-employee relationship allows—like tenderness, intimacy, and love.

He fills the jar with water, whistling Luke Combs' "Forever After All," and I want to believe he's thinking about the dance floor, too.

As if reading my mind, he observes, "Crazy to think where we were last night versus now." A big grin captures his lips.

I nod, looking down to hide the immediate pink that rises to my cheeks. Fortunately, he doesn't notice, busying himself with setting up things for dinner.

Nash sets the flowers at the center of the table before pulling out plates and silverware. He finds a couple of candles, places them on the table, and lights them. Next, he grabs two rustic glasses, filling them with red wine he opens before placing the rest of the bottle by the bouquet.

"Do you really want me drinking on the job?" I ask, never one to overindulge but still second-guessing myself in this new arrangement.

"I think you and I both deserve a glass of wine after the day we've had. But if you prefer not to, that's up to you, which obviously goes without saying."

I stare at the table apprehensively, biting my lower lip. I've only known Nash for a week, but I could fall in love with this cowboy and the sense of domesticity we're creating together. The constant companionship of someone thinking about me is better than I ever could have imagined.

"You and Ambrose deserve nothing but the best." He turns to the little guy seated in his new high chair, gnawing on a baby teething cracker. "Does this meet your standards, little buckaroo?"

I've never heard him speak so warmly to the baby, and it melts my heart. *Little buckaroo.* Seeing the rugged cowboy converse attentively with his nephew undoes all my best-laid plans for not getting attached to this duo.

A child-like part of me wants to grab my luggage and make a run for it before things get any more complicated. But the mature side knows there's no going back. I gave Nash my word, and I'm standing by it. Nevertheless, nothing about this arrangement is going to be easy.

Nash's vivid green eyes meet mine, overflowing with sizzling heat. My heart thuds against my ribs, and I feel happily lightheaded. "And does it meet your standards, Sparky?"

"It's a gorgeous setup, Nash. Thank you."

A pleased grin captures his face from ear to ear. "Good," he says, putting his head down and striding from the kitchen. Hollering back over his shoulder, he excuses, "Dinner smells like it's close. I'm going to get washed up."

I don't trust my voice to respond. Instead, I whisper raw-voiced to Ambrose, "Your uncle is some man. You'd do well to grow up and be just like him, the ramblin' part and the Texas accent aside."

❧

"Dunno, Okie. I grill a pretty mean steak, but this meal is down-home perfection."

"Down-home perfection? I'll take that as a compliment."

"It's not a compliment, Sparky. It's just fact. A compliment would be something like..." His slow drawl trails away for a moment as my heart and breath wait for his next pronouncements. "Something like ... the glow of the candlelight dancing across your face undoes me in the most painful, soul-stirring way."

I knit my brows, trying to control my accelerated breathing. "Just as an example?"

He brings his napkin to his lips, blotting his mouth. "Question is, how would you take it if it were more than an example?"

"Employer, employee," I remind.

He shakes his head, looking down at his plate and chuckling. "And temporary, to boot," he adds, nodding toward Ambrose, who's happily making a mess of the slab of mashed potatoes and butter I dolloped on his blue baby plate. Half of it covers his face, making him look like a miniature version of Santa, white beard and all. "Sorry if I need reminders. But this feels good. Better than anything I've experienced before."

"How do you mean?"

Nash pauses for a long moment, running his hand through his thick, brown hair. "I'll spare you the gory details, but I imagine you've already guessed I don't come from the most upstanding people. I mean, with my sister abandoning her baby and all. That's the tip of the iceberg, though," he says, eyeing me.

My face softens as I listen, attempting to understand the man beneath all the rodeo accolades and rough facades.

"It doesn't help that you keep looking at me like you genuinely care about what I have to say," he delivers the last sentence with an accusatory edge.

"Well, of course, I care about what you have to say," I reply. "Why wouldn't I?"

"Because nobody cares about a guy like me—not the deep down parts of me anyway. They're only interested in what I can do for them."

The corners of my mouth turn up skeptically. "Please, Nash. You were a rodeo champ. I imagine you had your pick of the ladies, too."

He sits back in his chair, making the ancient wood structure squeak for want of fresh glue. "They were interested in my talents and accomplishments. What I could do. How I could make money. But that went away the moment I started failing in competitions." He snaps his fingers for effect. "Poof! Gone with the smoke of my incinerated career. But you give me the strange impression that you're interested in *me* and *my feelings*. I'm not really used to it, and I'm not sure how to feel about it."

"I'm sorry if I make you feel uncomfortable," I excuse, starting to push back from the table.

But his hands come palms up to stop me. "No, it's fine. I kind of like it, honestly. I'm just afraid that I'm somehow misreading your interest, and if I really confide in you, it'll scare you away."

My eyes pan from Ambrose back to the handsome cowboy. "Does it look to you like I scare easily?"

"Maybe not," he retorts, shifting how he sits in the chair. "But you made it very clear at the wedding that you want nothing to do with cowboys."

I nod. "Because so many of them can't make up their mind or settle down. What's the use of tangling with that?"

"Fun, I imagine." His eyes get a mischievous glow.

I shake my head, frowning. "Not my idea of fun."

"I almost forgot," he observes, straightening in his chair and eyeing my purity ring. "You're one of *those* girls."

"And what do you mean by those girls?" I ask, arching an eyebrow.

"The settling down type."

"You already know that."

He nods, looking more than a little disappointed.

Nash has picked the wrong topic to challenge me on. Passion fills my voice as I retort, "It seems like this country is in the middle of an epidemic of men who don't want to grow up or commit. The disease has hit ropers and riders especially hard. But beautiful things like Ambrose don't happen ... Well, at least they may not reach their full potential without two people putting their childishness and selfishness aside and playing the long game."

Nash swallows hard, his face darkening. "The right man will be lucky to have you. Lucky beyond his wildest dreams."

"If he's grown up enough to figure it out," I counter, scowling.

"He will. When the time's right, he will."

"How can you be so sure?" I ask, trying to wrap my head around this amorphous conversation.

"Because he'll have done enough roaming in his life to know a good thing when he sees it. A thing too good to pass up."

"Says the inveterate bachelor." I chuckle.

Nash's eyes capture mine, an intensity in them that I can't decipher. "Some people aren't cut out for relationships and all the love and commitment that comes with them. I wouldn't know what to do with myself or how to act. Not after an upbringing where the household dogs and horses were more wanted than I was."

I try to keep my face free of judgment or reaction, but his words wound me to the core. I can't imagine growing up feeling that way. But I can't shake the feeling he needs to talk about this and process these emotions so that he can do better with Ambrose. So, despite the inherent danger of diving into a deeply intimate conversation with the cowboy, I prompt, "Tell me about your childhood."

He pushes away from the table, leaning back some more and putting his hands behind his head. He brings his left leg up, resting his calf over his knee. "Mama hated Dad and resented us kids. Not entirely sure why, but she skedaddled the first chance she got. I don't think I was more than six. My paternal grandparents lived up in Montana, and they kept trying to make arrangements for Dad, Nell, and me to move up there. But the more they pushed, the angrier Dad got until that became an estranged relationship, too. I suppose drink had something to do with it, as well as his lifestyle. The man wasn't cut out for kids, which left Nell and me constantly fending for ourselves. I'm not joking when I say he showed the ranch animals more attention than he did us, and he fed them better, too. I'll spare you the details, but he could transform from neglectful to physically abusive in a heartbeat." Nash shifts uncomfortably in his chair. "I've got a whole mess of scars to prove it. Sadly, I've also got his genes and blood. I suppose it's in my nature to be a bad parent and partner, though a growing part of me wants to do better than my old man. That said, there's only one thing I know for sure when it comes to things of a domestic nature."

"And what's that?"

"I'm an exceptional lover."

My cheeks burn, and I shake my head. "You and every other cowboy in Texas. But what sets you apart from the pack, Nash?"

He narrows his eyes.

Moving past his last flirtation, I continue in impassioned tones, "Bad parenting isn't something passed down genetically. It's conditioning. Which means you can either choose to make the same choices as your father or rise above your past and do better."

"Do you really believe in stuff like that, Sparky?" he asks, swallowing loudly.

"I believe that if you want something badly enough, there's nothing that can stop you from getting it. I looked up your PRCA stats, and your bronc riding career proves it. You don't get rankings like that without full commitment."

Nash sits up, crossing his arms over his chest. "And look where all that dedication got me. I never won the championship, and that last year of riding was pathetic. It proved people like me, with roots like mine, can never get ahead. Maybe it's for the best."

"It only proves one thing," I reply firmly, lifting my chin in a challenge. "That injuries suck."

"Shoot, look at me now," he says, frowning. "Repeating the same tired, old patterns. Getting neck-deep in the kind of trouble that could get me fired from my dream job *and* flirting with the nanny." His face hardens over the last observation before he stands.

"Don't worry. This nanny will only let you get in so much trouble."

"I'm figuring that out. You're no fun, Okie," he mutters like a spoiled adolescent.

"Men aren't looking for fun. Little boys are," I counter, making him grimace.

"A little boy *and* a baby? Dang, girl, you've really got your nanny work cut out for you. Maybe you should charge me double."

"Maybe I will. At least, for cooking and more than likely cleaning."

"I can take care of myself."

"So you say."

"As enlightening as this conversation has been, it's time for me to clean up and hit the hay. Let me help you clear plates first, though."

"Well, you're quite the optimist," I observe, my mind still stuck on his previous statements.

"How so?" he asks to the clink of the plates and silverware he collects.

"This will be Ambrose's first night in completely new surroundings. I don't know what kind of mom Nell was. But it's likely setting in right about now that she's not coming back for him anytime soon. It could be a rough adjustment—"

"Which means?"

"A sleepless night."

"Maybe for you." The cowboy laughs. "But I've got to be up at the crack of dawn for work. I can't put up with any baby fussing, and I won't. Besides, you've got every gadget in the book and then some to keep him quiet. And if all else fails, you two can sleep in the truck. I'll leave my keys on the hook by the front door."

My eyebrows shoot up into my hair. "More like you can sleep in the truck if we're too loud for you."

"Woman," he scolds, holding the plates and silverware and staring at me long and hard. "Need I remind you I'm paying you well? It's time for you to get some of that Mary Poppins nanny magic going."

"Mary Poppins nanny magic?" I chuckle, an exasperated edge to my voice. The man has perfected the art of alternating between kind and vulnerable versus hard-edged and rude. He's taken me through so many emotions in one brief conversation. I feel like we've gotten together, fallen in love, and broken up in less than an hour. It's exhausting, and it makes me rue why God made him such physical perfection. If only looks were enough.

Chapter Nine

NASH

Your uncle is some man. You'd do well to grow up and be just like him, the ramblin' part and the Texas accent aside.

I didn't mean to eavesdrop on Naomi, but I heard her say this to Ambrose earlier when he was in the high chair. It has my head spinning now. Considering how the conversation went after that, I doubt she still feels these sentiments. But the thought of her believing I'm the kind of man to look up to, even for little more than an hour or two, makes me want to do better.

So does the fact that the Okie shot every one of my overtures clean out of the water without hesitation. I usually have a better track record with women. But it seems like the pretty blonde is impervious to the charms that draw most women to me.

I'd be lying if I claimed I didn't want Naomi, though. And whatever else comes with her ... *maybe.* The problem with domesticity remains my fear of committed long-term relationships, especially with children. And Naomi strikes me as a woman who wants kids, though we still have so much to discuss and learn about each other.

Problem is, I don't have the wherewithal or patience for a family, even though playing house with Sparky has awakened a desperate need in me. One I've never felt before for any woman. She's everything I want. Attentive, affectionate, sassy, strong, and the kind of innocent that urges me to jealously protect her from the world.

What I wouldn't give to wake up with my arms wrapped around the beauty. To nuzzle her neck and tease her awake with featherlight kisses that run the length of her jawline to her cleft chin and then down her neck into places I can't allow myself to imagine without my heart exploding in my chest.

I'm starting to think she's like the PRCA Saddle Bronc Riding Championship. Something I hunger for desperately because of her unattainability. Of course, the only way to solve this problem is to have her, an impossibility by her own standard. It creates a vicious cycle of need that grows with each conversation, each look, each interaction passing between us. Like a coyote noose, tightening around my neck with each movement to try to slip free.

Doggone! Maybe I should give up my job at Heart's Desire Ranch altogether and return to Texas. As much as I love Colorado, nothing's going right for me, and...

"Wahhhhhhhhhhhhhhhhh..."

For crying out loud! *Seriously?!?*

"Wahhhhhhhhhhhhhhhhh..."

I scrub my hands over my face, shifting uncomfortably on the too-narrow, too-short couch. I resigned myself to a fitful night of sleep the moment I laid down. I could do better in the bed of my pickup truck with a sleeping bag. Hey, now that I think about it, it's not a half-bad idea.

"Wahhhhhhhhhhhhhhhhh..."

"Naomi!" I call out.

No answer apart from Ambrose's obnoxious screaming.

I grab my pillow, covering my head with it. This is unbearable. A man can't live like this.

"Shut him up!" I warn, turning onto my side. What in the heck was I thinking this afternoon at CPS when I decided to keep the rugrat? I was all up in arms about feeling like an unwanted child. Well, maybe *this* is why Dad wanted nothing to do with Nell and me.

"Wahhhhhhhhhhhhhhhh..."

"For the love of God, make him stop crying, Naomi, or I'll send both of you out to the pickup."

The pretty blonde appears in the doorway to the bedroom holding Ambrose, her eyes so groggy they keep shutting on their own. I don't know why I thought she'd be okay with Ambrose's fussing. But she looks even more tired than me. Maybe she's right. Maybe I am selfish and childish, and it's time to grow up.

"You look like heck, Okie."

She works hard to round her eyes at me. "It's three-thirty in the morning. I feel like it, too."

"You mean, you're as tired as I am?"

"Tex, you have asked me some ridiculous questions before. But no offense, that was plain stupid."

"Grumpy, too. I kind of like it."

She frowns. "Take him," she orders flatly, padding in my direction.

I sit up on the couch. "Oh no."

"Oh, yes."

"Woman, this is your job. I'm not getting paid for this," I reply frantically, totally ill-equipped, as she hands Ambrose to me, the kid writhing and angry in my arms as I place him on my shirtless chest.

Almost instantly, the little guy quits crying, and I feel like a fake dad trying to act like the real thing. As they say, though, fake it 'til you make it. And the faking appears to be working.

Speaking to the silence, Naomi says, "There. You're doing great. You're a natural."

"No, I'm not."

"Nash, how many orphaned calves or foals have you raised?"

She has a point which inspires my silence. So does the hungry way Naomi eyes my bare chest, her cheeks glowing anew.

Swallowing loudly, my nanny retorts, "That's what I thought. Try to channel some of the patience you'd afford them for your nephew."

"More like a son if my irresponsible, loser sister has her way," I grumble.

Silence. Despite my disgust over everything about this situation, my heart warms and melts for the little guy so peacefully positioned on my chest. There's something soothing about holding him that feels a lot like how people describe love.

Naomi calls groggily from the kitchen. "I'm warming up some formula." She yawns audibly. "Are you giving him a pacifier? Or how'd you get him to quiet down so much?"

Clearing my throat, I say, testily, "You'll have to see for yourself."

When Sparky enters the room sleepily holding the bottle, the light from the kitchen streams into the living room enough for her to make out Ambrose fast asleep on my bare chest.

She covers her mouth with her hand, standing speechless for a long moment. "Okay, that is the most adorable sight I've ever seen."

"So, you like my chest and abs?" I tease wickedly.

She shrugs. "They're alright. What I like is how sweet and nurturing you're being with Ambrose. You look like a daddy."

Daddy. There's that word again. Clearing my throat, I venture, "It's kind of how you look when you're singing to Ambrose ... like his mama. The most beautiful mama a boy could ever ask for."

"Did you hit more of that wine after Ambrose and I went to bed?" Naomi teases, pushing my blankets to the side to sit down on the couch next to us.

"Are you ready for this guy?" I whisper, feeling the little tike stir at the rumble of my voice.

She nods, her face open and love-filled, and something breaks inside me. Something that brings the walls I've spent so many years building crashing down around me. I can't ignore my feelings anymore.

I want Naomi Donovan. I've wanted her all week, and it's not the kind of wanting an irresponsible night or two could ever satisfy. Although I'd still like to try for argument's sake.

But, no, I'm afraid there's a lot more here. The kind of want whole lifetimes couldn't satiate. The kind of want that scares the heck out of me.

Tears fill my eyes inexplicably, and I hand her Ambrose, standing up quickly and pacing away to stand by the cabin window. I pull back the curtain, feigning looking outside. I can only hope she didn't notice the emotion in my expression.

"I'm truly sorry about this. I know you have a long day at work tomorrow, and I don't want to impact that—"

I hold up a hand to stop her, shaking my head and rubbing the back of my neck. Forcing myself to speak, to be a man instead of a boy, I say, "What's one hard work day compared to an abandoned kid missing his mother? I'll be fine. It's Ambrose you should be worried about."

"You know you did a really good job of comforting him while I was working on formula," Naomi observes. "He calmed right down for you. He trusts you, Nash."

"Not sure why," I grumble. "If you weren't here, I'd put a

pillow over my head and ignore the crying. Or better yet, lock him in the truck in his car seat to wail it out alone."

"You would not do that," Naomi scolds.

"And how do you know that?" I question, arching my eyebrow.

"Because you would've already done it instead of hiring me as a nanny."

I turn, folding my arms. "But what if I hired you for selfish reasons?"

"Well, of course, you did. But selfishness isn't always a bad thing. You knew your limits, so you brought me on to fill the care gaps you knew you couldn't provide."

"What if I did it to see you again?" I ask, stony-voiced.

Naomi chuckles, shaking her head.

"What?"

"Can you ever have a conversation that doesn't make me cycle through the full range of emotions? Or at least one that gets us to a new spot instead of circling back around to the same thing over and over again?"

"Come again?"

"It's always one step forward and two steps back with you. It's exhausting, and it's way too early for this." Sparky sets the empty bottle on the table next to her, putting Ambrose on her shoulder and patting his back until the little bundle lets out some surprisingly loud burps.

I chuckle, joking, "I finally see the family resemblance you've been talking about."

"No way. I don't buy that for one minute. You were nothing but polite with perfect table manners at dinner tonight."

"That's 'cause Dad would just as soon break a finger or backhand me for smacking or chewing with my mouth open. And elbows on the table? Or burping?" I shiver. "I still remember the pain from those whippings."

"That's terrible," Naomi says softly. "But could you ever imagine doing that to Ambrose when he gets older? Or Maddie? Or Gregory?"

Maddie is the ten-year-old daughter of Chase, the owner of Heart's Desire Ranch. And Gregory is right around the same age, the son of Portia, one of the guests at the wedding who Randall has been covertly wooing.

I stop for a moment, scrunching my face and truly thinking through Naomi's question. After a long pause, I confess, "No, I can't imagine using my physical strength against any kid of any age."

"You're not like your dad, then."

"Maybe not, but that doesn't mean I'm cut out for this whole fatherhood thing, either," I counter, running my hand through my hair.

Naomi beams at me. "One day at a time. Now, would you mind taking Ambrose from me, hopefully without waking him, and carrying him back to the crib?"

"Yes, ma'am." I approach her, never taking my eyes off her face. Her gaze remains uninterrupted in my direction, too. I can feel the electricity sizzling through the air between us as I reach down gently. My fingers accidentally graze over her warm, soft flesh and silky nightgown as I carefully pick up Ambrose, feeling him shift and fuss but fall instantly back to sleep on my chest as I saunter towards the bedroom.

I can feel Naomi behind me as I lean forward to place him gently in the playpen sleeper. Her lilac, vanilla, and honey fragrance envelopes me as she draws closer. I straighten, turning towards her and realizing she's far closer than I anticipated.

I don't know if it's utter exhaustion or unbridled need that directs my next move, but I draw her unhesitatingly and unrepentantly into my arms, covering her mouth with mine for a kiss so sweet, my head swims.

Her arms come up, clutching my neck, and her dainty fingertips slide into my hair, sending delicious shivers of desire up and down my spine. Her lips are inviting and warm, sweet like honey, and she sighs gently, parting them. My heart hammers against my ribs as I sweep into her mouth, claiming her with a fervency that's built to a fevered pitch over the course of this past week.

Wrapping my arms around her waist and pulling her demandingly against me, I fist the satiny fabric of her nightgown, relishing the feel of her soft, supple curves against my hard, angular planes. Desire floods her next sigh as I palm her cheek, changing the angle of my head and deepening my stroke.

If we could stick purely to things of a sexual nature, I'd admit I'm already head-over-heels in love with this woman. But I hold back, a sliver of doubt about my capacity to commit wedged between our eager bodies like a shard of ice. As my hands wander lower into more interesting territory, she stiffens, her lips tightening as she pulls her head back a couple of inches to glare into my face.

"Tex, I'm not that kind of girl. So, I'd appreciate it if you put your hands back on my hips."

"Darling, you're going to kill me," I sigh, complying and dropping my mouth to her soft neck.

"If I haven't made it clear enough yet, cowboy, I'm a ring-and-babies kind of woman. Not an it-was-fun-while-it-lasted girl."

"In other words, you're going to make me pay for my pleasure?" I murmur, pulling my head back and scowling at her.

"No, but I have half a mind to make you pay for that comment." She shrugs out of my grip, the muscles in her face straining with anger.

"But, Sparky," I whisper. "You've got me tied in knots, and I don't know what to do about it."

"Yes, you do know what to do about it. You just don't want to. And I'm not sure I want you to want to with how confusing you make everything."

"Wait, what?"

Her eyes bore into me, making it clear her answer is a no-answer.

Pacing back and forth, I run my fingers through my hair again. "Why God would make a spitfire like you, I'll never know. You're going to be the death of me."

"No, stubbornness is going to be the death of you," she hisses, pushing me towards the bedroom door. "Sweet dreams, Tex."

"Is that it? You're done with me so soon?" I let her push me into the doorway before standing firm. The moment the blonde realizes she can't budge me even an inch, her face flushes red, and fire flashes in her eyes. Dang, I love this woman angry.

"Good night and good riddance. I need to shut the door."

"No," I drawl. "You need to give me one more last-chance kiss."

"Last chance?"

"I know you, Sparky, and tomorrow you're going to act like this never should've happened and never will happen again. But that's not going to work for me."

She puts her hands on her hips, pressing her lush, pink lips into a thin line. "Then, what do you suggest?" she asks imperiously, arching her gorgeous dark blonde eyebrows.

"A negotiation," I growl, stepping closer to her and wrapping my arms back around her. Despite the vitriol she directs towards me, Naomi melts in my arms. It gives me all the confirmation I need that these feelings of mine are fully, passionately requited.

I close the distance between us slowly, this time savoring the closeness of our lips a mere half an inch apart, her warm breath shed on my face. My hands slide up her back to her shoulders, palming her delicate décolletage and running my fingers lightly across her collarbones, neck, and jawline until her face is rose scarlet, and her body shivers.

Naomi's lips capture mine frantically, and I chuckle as her tongue claims me, all warm velvet that melts my heart like wax in my chest. Her arms thread around my neck, and she whispers as she kisses me again and again, "You. Are. Insufferable." Capturing my mouth with another passionate flourish, she makes my insides quiver. The woman knows how to kiss. My self-control flounders as she pushes me backward through the door.

This is it! Everything I've been dreaming about since I first laid eyes on the Oklahoma babe. And a smart move on her part. The couch or the living room floor may not be as comfortable as her bed, but we'll figure it out away from Ambrose...

Suddenly, she pulls away, sliding back through the door and closing it on my face. I hear the lock turn, and she whispers seductively, "Dream on, Tex. I'm still not that kind of girl."

I let my head fall back, chuckling in low, gravelly tones. This woman is going to be my literal undoing. God help me!

"You're killing me, Okie."

"Goodnight," she adds in scolding tones.

Silence. I shake my head, standing there longer than I care to admit before finally giving up.

I'm pathetic. Her lapdog. The woman owns me. And it's scary as heck because *this* has never happened to me before. *Why does it feel so good?*

I return to my dissatisfying spot on the couch, my head swimming and my lips still savoring the warmth and sweetness of her touch.

If she keeps this up, I'll be ring shopping before the end of the week. Naomi's got me wrapped as tightly around her finger as Ambrose has her wrapped around his chubby digit. *This* is worse than no good. It's impossible. But never has impossible looked, tasted, sounded, smelled, or felt so dang tantalizing.

Chapter Ten

NAOMI

Thankfully, Nash is long gone by the time Ambrose's baby noises awaken me. He coos gently in his crib, lost in a baby world that I wish I could understand. My eyes dart to the digital alarm clock next to my bed. Six twenty-seven in the morning.

"Not bad, Mr. Ambrose. Once we got you over the three a.m. hump, you did okay," I observe, stretching. Three a.m. It hits me all at once.

The manly smell of Nash's cypress and sandalwood cologne, the feel of his impossibly soft, warm lips moving over mine. The way he boldly claimed my mouth and then tried to follow suit with my body. My cheeks burn at the lengths I went to, to stop him, self-control hanging by a few frayed threads.

I can't let myself get in that situation again with the cowboy. It's a road to ruin and heartbreak ... unless he decides to change. But those changes would need to be monumental for me.

After all, I need a man ready for commitment and to lead a family, not one still toying with the bachelor life. I won't hold my breath. Besides, when did a woman pining away for a man to change ever work?

Despite the temptation, the man's gorgeous looks, and his sexy confidence, I absolutely refuse to betray myself in that way. I have standards. I have boundaries, and I won't let anybody tread on them. I haven't let men in the past, and I'm not about to now. After all, I've had enough friends who caved to a man's desires only to get left high and dry. I won't make that concession. Not even for the world's hottest cowboy.

Ambrose, however, is an entirely different matter. I reach into the playpen sleeper to pull him out, making a goofy face. His blue eyes round as he recognizes me, smiling and laughing. I am in love. One hundred percent a goner.

"If only your uncle could be as sweet and guileless as you are. Not saying there's anything wrong with him. He's quite a man. If he could ever figure out what he actually wants."

Never gonna happen, Naomi. Don't kid yourself. Instead of worrying about the gorgeous cowboy, I dive into creating a schedule for Ambrose, making notes on my phone about time and activity as we move through what feels like a natural progression for the day.

After his morning feeding and burping, I set him up in the high chair with some strawberry yogurt, mashed banana, and little pieces of sugar-free baby cereal that look like Cheerios.

The result is an utter mess. The kind I should have put a tarp down for, but it gives him a chance to explore the world through touch and taste in safe ways. It lets him work on honing his hand-eye coordination and finger dexterity.

I snap countless photos of the little guy covered in food, laughing at the adorable images. While he plays in the mess in his high chair, I straighten up the kitchen, humming. My mind wanders back to those passionate kisses with Nash, and I can't think straight.

The chemistry zinging between us was real, palpable, and

shockingly urgent for a woman who prides herself on chastity before marriage. It hasn't been an easy decision, especially in this day and age. But I want what my parents have, and I want to claim the blessings God has for me by doing things right. Luna, my bestie, has always marveled at my resolve, but I feel temptation getting the better of me with Nash. Is this what happens with the right guy?

I chuckle to myself. *Right guy?* Now, there's a ridiculous thought.

Luna tried to explain it to me with Ledger. How hard it was to wait until their wedding night, but I hope they were happy they did. There's nothing I wouldn't give to hear my bestie's voice right now and to update her on everything that's going on. But I would never interrupt her honeymoon.

After the kitchen's spic and span, I grab a big towel, wrap Ambrose and his mess in it, and head for the bathroom. My heart warms as I notice Nash must've set up the baby bathtub in the bottom of the shower after taking his this morning. It doesn't help that this cabin is so small that Nash and I have to share a bathroom, and he has to sleep on the couch. Fortunately, his work schedule will keep us apart most of the time.

Setting Ambrose gently on the floor with the towel under him. I draw a warm bath, getting the water high enough for him to splash. Still, I know enough from having younger siblings to never leave him alone in the bathtub. I put on some gentle music while he enjoys the water, playing and laughing.

When his chubby fingers start to prune up, I grab a washcloth, washing him gently with the brand-new baby soap we bought last night. Then, I dry him off with fluffy towels, slather him in non-toxic, organic, fragrance-free lotion, and head into the bedroom to diaper and dress him for the day.

His blond curls form tight ringlets that I can't take enough pictures of. I hesitate about whether to text a couple to Nash, not wanting to fan the flames of anything unwanted.

But I relent, reminding myself I'm still the nanny, and he and Ambrose have a lot yet to learn about each other. Someday, I'll likely be out of the picture, but these two will be family for life.

I get no response from the texts, which doesn't surprise me. After all, the ranch is spotty when it comes to signals, and he seems like the type of man who doesn't like to be distracted at work.

Ambrose goes in his playpen with the mobile on and toys to play with, and I call my mom, hungry for advice. She answers on the first ring, "Nana—" That's the nickname my parents and Luna sometimes use for me. "What was your cryptic message about being stuck in Colorado yesterday? I tried to call, but you didn't pick up."

Putting her on speaker, I flip back through my calls from yesterday, seeing I failed to return ones from her and Luna. Now, I feel guilty. "Sorry, Mama. But yesterday completely got away from me. So much happened. I don't even know where to start."

"Then, start in the middle," she says, falling back on her plainspoken wisdom.

I inhale slowly as if I'm about to deep dive into the Atlantic. "Okay, so as I was saying in texts yesterday, my flight kept getting canceled because of afternoon thunderstorms. And so, I was trying to figure out whether I was going to rent a car and drive back to California or sleep in the airport and hope for a better flight tomorrow."

"Wait, why were you going to sleep in the airport?"

I exhale sharply, hating to admit this. "Because I'm more or less out of the money I budgeted for the wed—"

"You should have asked Daddy and me."

"Mama, I'm giving this adulting thing a really hard try. And that means bailing myself out when problems arise."

"But, baby girl, you will always be our daughter, and we

don't want anything to happen to you. You should've called. Do you want Daddy and me to start looking for flights to Oklahoma City? We could get you settled here and away from California once and for all."

They've been on this one for months now. Yes, taxes would be cheaper, but tornado-hopping? It was never my favorite hobby. Fortunately, Colorado represents a fantastic third option. At least temporarily, which brings me to the point of my call. "Actually, I'm relocating to Colorado for a while to be by Luna and Ledger."

"Ohh!" Mama exclaims, her voice a mixture of relief and disappointment.

"Yeah. Things happened kind of unexpectedly, but I've already got a full-time job and a place to stay. So, it's like God has paved the way for this..."

"And?"

"There's just one minor problem, but I'll figure it out."

"And what's that?"

I bite my bottom lip, trying to sound nonchalant. "My boss is a former saddle bronc rider on the PRCA. Dad may know him, Nash Carter—"

Before I can say another word, Mama's got her hand over the phone, hollering towards my dad. "Honey, do you know of a Nash Carter? A bull rider or something?"

"Saddle bronc rider," I correct, but she can't hear me.

"Carter? Nash Carter? Hmm... Oh, you mean that bronc buster guy who broke his back on live TV a year and a half ago? Is he still alive?"

I grimace at the rundown.

"Baby girl," Mama says into the receiver. "Did you hear what Daddy said?"

"Ouch!" I say.

She questions, "Are you telling me this Carter guy is still alive?"

"Yes, Mama. Like I said, he's kind of my boss now—"

Her hand goes back over the receiver, relaying everything to Daddy. "Her boss?" he protests. "Don't tell me she's getting into rodeoing or something."

Mama comes back on the line. I fight the urge to walk her yet again through the steps of putting somebody on speakerphone. It always ends in a hangup rather than a family-wide call.

"No, I'm not getting into rodeoing." I chuckle. "I'm nannying his baby full-time. His name is Ambrose, and he's the cutest thing. Let me send you some pictures." I put her on speaker as I go back through the more than fifty images I've already shot just this morning, sending her a few.

"Oh, my goodness! He's adorable! And what is Mrs. Carter like?"

"There is no Mrs. Carter." I peek into the playpen, breathing a sigh of relief at the sight of Ambrose with closed eyes, relaxing into sleep.

"No, Mrs. Carter? What do you mean?"

"Well, Ambrose, the baby, is actually Nash's nephew. His sister abandoned him on Nash's bunkhouse doorstep yesterday. He was originally going to surrender him to CPS, but then he relented when he found out there was no placement for the baby. Fortunately, my flight got canceled, and so it worked out for me to help."

Daddy's voice hollers plain as day in the background. "Ladies man as I remember. Always surrounded by cowgirls. You tell Nana to watch herself around a guy like that."

Mama whispers into the phone, "Daddy says he's a less than scrupulous man. Wait, you're not living in the same house, are you?"

"Well, that's what nannies do, Mama. Don't worry. We have separate sleeping arrangements. Well, I mean, obviously."

"Baby girl, I know how the world views things of this

nature, but don't forget how we raised you or what the good Lord expects. Besides, any man worth his salt wouldn't think twice about committing to you for life. I know you've been having trouble finding that in California. And I imagine it might be the same in Colorado. That whole West Coast is wild, Nana. Come home to Oklahoma. There are plenty of nice guys here. Why..." She launches into a diatribe about young, single men at their church, but all I can think about is Nash.

What in the world is wrong with me? Suddenly, I hear beeping in the background. Looking down at my phone, I see that Luna's calling me. "Mama," I interrupt. "I have to answer this call. It's Luna."

"Oh, Luna? Alright, well, call me back later. I'm going to be a mess of worry until I hear from you again."

"I promise. Bye, Mama."

I click over. "Luna!"

"Nana, I'm so glad I got a hold of you! I tried calling yesterday, but I figured you were already on your plane."

"Funny thing," I say, chuckling. "I'm still in Ouray."

"Still in Ouray? Let me guess. Afternoon thunderstorms?"

"That was the catalyst, you could say. But then, I got this job offer I couldn't pass up."

"Job offer? Do tell."

"I've taken a full-time job as a nanny for one of the ranch hands at Heart's Desire Ranch."

Silence seizes the line until I'm certain I've lost Luna's signal. Finally, she asks, "Which one? I didn't know any of them had a baby. Although I wasn't really paying attention to any of that."

"Nash. The cute one."

"The cute one?" Luna echoes. "Wait, why do you sound so excited? Doesn't that mean he's got a wife or, at the very least, a baby mama?"

I chuckle. "No, Nash is the baby's uncle. Apparently, his sister, Nell, left baby Ambrose at the ranch bunkhouse yesterday morning."

"Huh." Luna doesn't sound too excited. "Why don't you stay at our place instead? Then, you won't have to worry about a baby. Besides, I imagine you'll be able to catch a makeup flight as soon as the weather's a little better."

"No, Luna, I'm thinking about staying in Ouray to be closer to you." And to see where things head with the bad-boy cowboy, though I'll never admit this out loud.

Luna lowers her voice. "But doesn't that mean you're living with Nash?"

"Yeah," I answer weakly. "But that's what nannies do. And he works all day anyway, so it's not like I'll see him much."

"You don't have to see him much to have trouble, Nana. Especially with the way he was looking at you all week and the way you were looking at him. And the things you said about him. I mean, you were on cloud nine every time you talked about the hunky cowboy."

"I promise. I'll be careful."

"Yeah, but under the same roof is hard. I mean, I could have never done that with Ledger, and I'm fully willing to admit a lot of it was my fault. I don't know what happens when you find the right person, but you want them to the depths of your soul, and it's very powerful and seductive. If Ledger wasn't such a gentleman and so respectful of me, I would've never ended up waiting."

"But are you glad that you did?" I ask, my voice straining.

"Yes. Absolutely. It was perfect. He's perfect. I've never been so in love in my entire life. I don't need to eat. I don't need to drink water. I don't need to sleep. I just need him."

"Wow."

"I know," she says with an embarrassed chuckle.

"It makes sense, though, because you guys are obviously soulmates."

"It didn't seem that way when we first met. At least, not from his side."

"Stop it, Luna. He loved you from the first moment he laid eyes on you in that blizzard. He didn't think he was good enough for you, though. Wild to think all of that was going on while I was getting rushed to Montrose by those search and rescue guys for surgery."

Luna sighs. "I was so worried about you. I still feel guilty over everything."

"No need to. I'm walking, and I have a savage life experience trophy to show for it—"

"Well, don't let this arrangement with Nash result in another life experience trophy. I've heard scars on the heart never really heal."

"Yeah, I'm sure Mama would say the same thing."

"You're the best woman I know, Nana, and you deserve all the happiness in the world. And the most amazing guy to ever walk this planet." She giggles. "Well, apart from Ledger, of course. Why don't you stay in the main ranch house with Chanel, Chase, and Maddie? They have more than enough rooms."

"That's another thought," I say, my voice and thoughts trailing away.

"And you have the door code to our cabin. Make yourself at home."

"Even with a baby?"

Luna chuckles. "Maybe when I get back, I can help you with your nannying duties. You know, Ledger and I would love to have babies, so I need to start honing my mama skills."

"Believe me, the learning curve is steep," I answer.

"Wahhhhhhhhhhhhhhhh..."

"Oh, shoot, I must've been too loud," I whisper as

Ambrose's high-pitched cry fills the room, gaining momentum. "I better go."

"Oh, that's the baby? I love that sound."

"Try loving it in the same room."

"Okay, I'll let you go. But send me pictures, okay? And make sure you stick to your guns with the cowboy. You deserve everything, Naomi, and that means not compromising your morals for anyone."

"I promise. Bye, babe," I say, ending the call and pocketing my phone before I reach into the playpen to retrieve Ambrose.

Chapter Eleven

NASH

"You look like road kill this morning," Randall "Rugged" Collier laughs, patting me on the back as I saunter into the stable, nodding at the other ranch hands.

"It was a long night," I grumble, still enveloped in a strange mixture of elation and rejection. I've never had a woman do to me what Naomi did at the door of the bedroom, and I don't know whether to find hope in her actions or despondency. I may seem tough and rugged on the outside. But if she's playing with my heart, it's really going to hurt.

I glare at the black cowboy with sunshine written on his face and joy animating his actions as he whistles and tacks up his mount for the day. "What's got you in such a good mood? You finally figured things out with that single mother you've been chasing?"

"Her name's Portia, and she's amazing," he says in rich tones, a wistfulness in his voice.

"Great! The whole ranch is in love except for me."

Rugged chuckles. "Don't act so fatalistic. The ranch

rumor mill's already talking a mile a minute about the pretty little blonde you hired on as a nanny. You've been making eyes at her all week, and everyone knows it."

"Yeah," I confess, removing my black Stetson and smoothing my hair. "But she's giving me mixed signals."

"Mixed signals?" Rugged asks, waggling his eyebrows.

"Basically, like Portia was giving you until yesterday when you apparently worked everything out."

"Well, I wouldn't say everything. But we did have a meeting of the minds and the hearts, and I'm going to marry that woman and raise Gregory as my own boy. That's going to happen."

"Your smile and good mood are obnoxious," I grumble with a frown.

"Only because you're not as lucky in love as I am. But in so many ways, it's up to you, Nash. Are you treating her right? Making your intentions clear?"

I stop combing my horse, putting my hands on my hips. "Making my intentions clear? How do I do that when I don't even know what my intentions are?"

"There's your problem," Rugged drawls. He spent years in Texas, and he's got the accent to prove it. Straight out of the Hill Country like me.

Chase and Eldon enter the stable, and I put my head down, getting back to work. I try not to draw too much attention to myself with the new boss and ranch foreman around. But Rugged has no such concerns. From what I've gathered, he and Chase grew up together in Ouray, and they've remained close like brothers.

"Morning, Gents, y'all ready for a long ride and some fence-mending?" Chase asks, projecting his deep baritone through the stable.

"Yes, sir," a chorus of male voices reply, none sounding too enthusiastic. That is, except for Rugged, who's still smiling from ear to ear.

"And how's the baby and the cabin?" Chase asks, coming over to stand by me.

"Fine, sir. I can't thank you enough for letting me stay there until I sort things out."

The corners of his mouth turn up, and he runs his hand over his brown beard pensively. His brows furrow. "It's come to my attention that you have a live-in nanny. Naomi Donovan from the wedding?"

"Yes, sir."

"Don't lay a finger on her, Carter."

"Come again?" I ask, stunned by his words.

Chase crosses his arms, frowning. "It's like Eldon told you when you started here. We'll have no drama with the ladies, and I know you, Cash. I watched you in the PRCA. You were nothing but trouble. You better have turned over a new leaf because Chanel considers Naomi a close friend, and she's not about to have you break her heart."

"She's more likely to break mine, sir," I admit before thinking better of it. I'm not trying to talk back, but it's the truth.

"Keep it that way, or I'll have to move Naomi and the baby up to the main ranch house. Believe me, you don't want to see me sleep-deprived because there's bawling in the house."

Eldon chimes in. "There'll be bawling soon enough anyway with the way your new bride loves babies."

Chase grumbles, "All the more reason why I need as much sleep as I can get while I can still get it."

Eldon and Chase laugh and joke back and forth as they head further down the stable to say hello to Raul, José, Dexter, and the rest of the guys.

I side-eye Rugged, breathing a sigh of relief. I thought for sure I'd lose my job when Ambrose showed up. But this crew's far more lenient than previous ones I've worked.

As if reading my mind, Rugged warns, "Don't mistake Chase's cordiality for weakness. He'll terminate you without a second thought if you step out of line. And with the missus concerned about Naomi? You better leave her the heck alone or put a ring on it. I don't see any in-between."

"I could hire a different nanny."

"Obviously."

"Or quit being so stubborn about keeping Ambrose. I should've left him at CPS in the first place. Kept myself out of this whole mess."

"But family's family, Nash."

"You're right," I admit. "And everybody needs family. It's like you told me when I started. I'll always feel like a part of the family at Heart's Desire Ranch. But what if I want to add another layer to that family with Naomi and Ambrose? Would it be so bad? I keep asking myself these questions, and the answers are clear. I want to take the next step, though I'm not quite sure what I'll be stepping into."

Rugged laughs. "Join the club. But something tells me heading off into the unknown will be entirely worth it. Maybe the greatest adventure either of us has ever been on." Rugged positions the saddle blanket on his horse before gently hauling the saddle into place slightly forward before settling it back.

I side-eye him, chuckling. "You really do have it bad for Portia, then."

"I do."

I confess, "Truth be told, I've got it bad for Naomi, too. I have all week, and I don't begin to know what to do about it because she's not like other girls. And most definitely not like any women I've ever met."

"What's different about her?"

I shrug, positioning my blanket and then the saddle.

"She's not impressed by me or my rodeo background in the least, and she's got these super strong boundaries. Won't take any guff from me, and she knows her mind and heart and speaks both freely."

"Terrifying." Rugged chuckles sarcastically.

"You asked."

"All the things that are different about her sound like reasons to keep her if she'd have a fool like you. What's the problem?"

I frown, looking down at the toes of my boots. "Until meeting her, I had convinced myself I wasn't cut out for the whole relationship and family thing. Of course, it was never much of a problem because I didn't have anything tempting me. The girls that surrounded me when I rodeoed made their motivations very clear. They liked me for my career, wealth, and good looks. And as soon as the first vanished, they didn't stick around to see the rest go. But Naomi's got me entertaining things I never thought possible."

"In other words, you weren't worried about losing the previous girls because you never had them in the first place," Rugged says, leading his horse out of the stable. I follow behind him with my mount in tow.

Is that what my problem is? I'm afraid of what losing Naomi could do to me, and so I'm unwilling to act. It's a realization that feels spot-on, even as it makes me question what's wrong with me. I've never been this messed up over a woman.

"If you saw the family I'm from, you'd understand why I'm struggling," I excuse, climbing into the saddle.

Rugged does the same before eyeing me fiercely. "Don't make excuses."

"If I can't make excuses about my awful upbringing, then what am I supposed to do?"

"Cowboy up, Nash," Rugged orders. "Besides, I'd put my family against yours any day. If it weren't for Eldon, my grandpa, and this ranch, who knows what would've happened to me. I was a delinquent who always took the trouble way out of things."

"But doesn't that make you hesitant with Portia and Gregory? Worried you won't be the man they need?" I ask, stroking my beard in contemplation.

"Every man worries about that at some point, Nash. But you know what separates the mice from the men?"

I shake my head, furrowing my brows. The way he's talking to me makes me feel like I'm twenty instead of thirty. But maybe it's what I need. After all, he's not the first person to allude to me in the last twenty-four hours that I have some growing up to do. And unlike other men, I've never had a father figure to have this conversation with.

Rugged narrows his eyes, his voice firm. "Men make it happen despite their fears while mice wallow in them."

"But how could I begin to know what I want with this girl when she's as staid as a Quaker? You can't commit to someone without ... you know."

Rugged chuckles, but there's a warning edge to it. "And how's that been working out for you, Tex? Are the girls lining up for commitment? Has all that lovey-dovey stuff clarified your thoughts and focused your mind on any one woman?"

He's got a point. One that leaves me genuinely puzzled.

"You look bumfuzzled. What's wrong?" Rugged asks.

"Bumfuzzled?" I shake my head. "I haven't heard that word in forever."

"It's the only way to describe the perplexed look on your face," he observes.

"More like pained," I grumble as the rest of the ranch hands file out of the stable, mounting their rides.

I side-eye Rugged, thankful for a long ride and hard work to clear my head and get me thinking straight again about what's going on with Naomi.

Rugged grunts, "Nash, you're currently on a one-way road to losing Naomi for sure. No matter what. You've got some thinking to do ... and course correction, to boot, if you want to turn things around and do right by her. But first, you've got to commit to one outcome."

I nod, frowning. He's not telling me anything I don't already know. But easier said than done.

Chapter Twelve

NAOMI

A truck engine rumbles, drawing closer as the sound of crushed gravel reaches my ears. My heart races, ready for the one thing I've wanted all day but been too stubborn to admit. I need to see Nash again.

"Ambrose, guess who's here," I say in sing-song tones to the baby on my hip, trying to act like my knees aren't weak and my body isn't trembling. Heavy footfalls precede the squeaky door and the entrance of the cowboy, backlit by late afternoon sunlight.

Dutifully removing his black Stetson and pressing it against his chest, he kicks the door shut before toeing off his boots and leaving them near the welcome mat. He holds another bouquet of lavender and butter-yellow blossoms, and his cheeks darken as he looks at me gravely.

"They're gorgeous, Nash."

"No, you're gorgeous," the dirt- and sweat-covered cowboy says, eyeing me nervously and clenching his jaw. "Now, if you'll excuse me, I better take a shower before you start smelling what I've been smelling all afternoon."

I take the flowers, letting myself savor the crackling of electricity that passes between our fingertips before he grabs his knapsack of clothes and beelines for the bathroom.

I head back into the kitchen, securing Ambrose in his baby swing and turning it on. I just fed, burped, and changed him, and I can tell he's ready for another little snooze before dinner. I replace the water in the Mason jar from last night, adding the additional flowers and admiring their untamed splendor.

As I start working on dinner, chicken piccata with penne tossed in pesto, I think about the second conversation I had with Mama this afternoon. The one where Daddy got on the phone and told me in no uncertain terms will one of his daughters live under the same roof as Nash Carter.

Of course, this brought out my stubborn streak and a reminder that I'm a twenty-four-year-old woman who knows how to take care of myself. In exasperated tones, Daddy said, "Promise me you'll look that cowboy up online. You need to know who you're mixing company with."

I couldn't argue with my dad since I know he has my best interests at heart. So, I watched old clips of Nash on YouTube, stuck somewhere between admiration and jealousy and getting a thorough education in my boss's philandering ways.

Every gorgeous rodeo queen on his arm made my heart simmer with envy. And his free-wheeling former life both intrigued and scared me. Could a rip-roaring bronc rider really be okay with settling down after a life lived so raucously? I have my doubts. But from what he's told me over the past couple of days, I also sense there was an emptiness in his former life. Maybe despite the glitz, glamor, and beauty, it wasn't as satisfying as it looked.

Logic tells me the living arrangement needs to change immediately. Like yesterday, but I rue the thought of having this conversation with Nash because I don't begin to know how he'll react. Or if I'll keep my job. The thought of leaving Ambrose breaks my heart, though I've been with him little more than twenty-four hours. And never seeing Nash again without exploring the possibilities? Though pragmatic, the ache in my chest tells me it's not what I want.

The smell of soap brings my attention to the entryway of the kitchen where Nash stands, his hair and beard damp from the shower. He stares past me at Ambrose in the swing, delighting at how the baby's eyes round, and he waves his hands and feet, cooing and smiling.

"Shoot," the cowboy says, sounding truly shocked. "It's like he recognizes me."

I giggle, remembering this morning and how happy it made me when I peeked in on Ambrose for the first time, and he reacted the same way. "That's because he does recognize you," I say, trying to hide the emotion in my voice as Nash approaches me.

I turn back towards the stove with my head down, over-whelmed by the sudden longing he awakens in me. I need a moment to pull myself back together. But Nash doesn't take the hint. Wrapping me in a bear hug from behind, he nuzzles my neck, whispering gently, "And you've been on my mind all day, Okie. Seems you've turned my brain into Swiss cheese."

I bite my bottom lip, trying not to melt into his arms and failing miserably. He kisses my cheek. "Dinner smells amazing. Can I help with anything?"

I shrug, working hard to catch my breath. "Maybe you could set the table again like last night?"

"I'm prepared to do everything again like last night," he says, chuckling against my cheek. "Except maybe Ambrose's three a.m. wakeup call, although I'd be lying if I said I didn't like the outcome of it."

"Mr. Carter, need I remind you I'm just the nanny?"

"Just the nanny?" he repeats gruffly. "No, ma'am. Before you agreed to this nannying gig, I was just a cowboy with a kid. But in little over a day, you've already become the beating, living heart of this home. Ambrose and I both know it. But enough. I know when to back off. Sorry, Sparky."

His words touch me to the core, flooding my mind, heart, and soul with so many raw needs and hopes. The dichotomy between the rodeo star I watched earlier and this man is downright confounding. Yet, as much as I fear getting hurt by him, I also find myself thirsting for more, disappointed when he walks away.

He unlatches Ambrose from the swing. Holding him up and gently twirling around. The baby giggles deep in his chest, a belly laugh that makes Nash stop and look at me. We both dissolve into surprised laughter.

I know better. Everyone I love most in this world has said their peace about my current situation, and I don't disagree with them. So, why does this feel so good with Nash and Ambrose? And why do I wish his words were true? That I really was the beating, living heart of this place?

Nash twirls around again, and Ambrose guffaws with joy. The cowboy echoes his amusement before they head towards the front door. Nash hollers over his shoulder, "Sparky, Ambrose and I are going for a little walk."

"Mind the mosquitoes," I call after them.

"They're nothing like they are in Texas or Oklahoma."

"Still."

"Yes, ma'am."

As sunset gives off its last glorious, golden rays, I peek through the front window at Nash and his nephew. He holds the baby tentatively still, dwarfing the little guy with his own height and size. Nevertheless, I see a new easiness between them that wasn't there yesterday.

Moreover, I catch a glimmer of something I need to see after a day of being non-stop warned about this man. Nash would make a good daddy. It's obvious. If he could ever be persuaded to settle down.

Persuaded. There's nothing romantic about that verb, and it doesn't reflect in any way the fairytale love stories I devoured as a kid. About valiant knights who risk anything and everything for the fair maiden. Without reservation or indecision. And with few expectations beyond a thank you smile or resting securely in the knowledge she's safe.

Sure, there's no reality in those stories. But it's still what I want. What most girls want, I'd imagine, as everything from romance novels to Hallmark movies and early Taylor Swift songs attest. Tough to give up the fantasy.

Still, there's something about seeing Nash and Ambrose like this that does inexplicable things to my heart and my head. The kind of things that make me want the impossible.

After I pile plates high with chicken piccata and pasta and carry them to the table, I head to the front door to call the boys. Nash looks up, his warm eyes devouring me as he rubs his stomach with his hand. "Did you hear that, Ambrose? Time for some grub."

Nash secures Ambrose in his high chair, and I put a few overcooked, soggy noodles on his tray to play with while we eat. I spent a good part of the day, when I wasn't researching Nash, reading up on introducing food and ways to make this discovery a tactile experience. The way the little guy furrows his brows in concentration, chasing the slippery noodles around the tray with his fingers, has the cowboy and me both laughing again.

"You've outdone yourself, Okie. If I'd known what a good cook you were, I would've added extra salary for your culinary pleasures."

I chuckle, cheeks burning at the word "pleasures," though I can't explain why. "It's not too late to renegotiate, you know."

"It is," he says, grabbing his fork and knife and diving into his meal.

I grab my wine glass, sipping nervously and feeling a lump rise in my throat. Despite everything I've learned about him and all the warnings, he's the most handsome man I've ever seen. So handsome I have trouble dragging my eyes away from him. I also savor the delight he takes in eating my food. Clearly, he's ravenous *and* impressed.

I pick at my own plate, my stomach twisting apprehensively. I can't let what happened last night continue. Even though the new physicality between us continued in front of the stove when he greeted me post-shower. And it was far from unwelcome.

"What's wrong?" Nash asks, furrowing his brows. "You've barely touched your food."

I open my mouth to speak and then close it again, glancing between Nash and Ambrose. We could be a family, all I've ever really wanted. This feels so good. Like something that needs to be protected and preserved. I can't ruin it because I'm fighting a losing battle with lust. "Nothing," I lie, shaking my head. "You know how sometimes when you cook, you don't feel like eating?"

"Never happened to me." The cowboy grins candidly, melting my heart some more. He grabs his glass, takes a sip of the Cabernet Sauvignon, and drops his eyes to the table. His face grows somber.

"I could ask you the same question."

"What?" he replies, looking up absentmindedly.

"I could ask you what's wrong, too."

Nash bites his bottom lip, running his big, work-hardened hand through his mahogany locks. "It's not that anything's wrong. It's that I'm trying to sort something out in my head."

"And what's that?" I ask breathlessly.

His emerald eyes snap to mine. "What's happening between you and me—"

My eyes flicker towards Ambrose for the millionth time

today, already obsessing over his well-being in ways I'm not used to, and I let out a strangled scream. The baby's face is going from deep red to purple, and his eyes are bugging out. He doesn't make a sound, but it's clear he's choking.

"Oh my God!" I hear my words from a distance, like they're disembodied, as I jump to my feet, tears springing to my eyes as a pit forms in my stomach.

Reflexively, I pull him out of his high chair, patting frantically on his back. Nothing. Not a sound. Silence.

I only have a split second to look up at Nash with pleading eyes before the cowboy grabs his nephew, placing him over one arm and slapping his back hard.

My hand comes to my mouth, certain he's going to hurt Ambrose but not knowing what else to do. His hand slams down over his back again. Hot tears pour down my cheeks, filling my mouth with the taste of salt.

"Wahhhhhhhhhhhhhhhh..." A chunk of noodle hits the floor.

Nash's eyes meet mine, and he lets out a long, relieved sigh. "Thank God," he says, pulling the infant into his arms and staring him in the face. "You scared the heck out of Sparky and me. Dang, kid!"

Elation and relief flood me, followed by inky, oppressive guilt. It's all my fault. He choked on a noodle. The seriousness of the game I'm playing hits me all at once. My face tightens with a violent sob, and I choke down the sound, staring wildly between Nash and Ambrose.

"I'm not cut out for this," my voice squeaks. "I almost killed him."

Nash's face floods with concern. "Nah, darling. It could've happened to anyone—"

"I don't know what I was thinking trying to be a nanny. I mean, I don't have the right training, and my experience with babies is so limited." I shake my head, pacing back and forth, animated by fear and shame. *What was I thinking when I agreed to this job?*

Voice failing me any further, I run into the back bedroom, shutting the door and jumping onto the bed. I bury my face in the pillows as a thousand emotions grip me simultaneously, and I wail at the thought of what nearly happened.

Behind me, I hear the door squeak open and a little coo from Ambrose. "Shh," Nash whispers. "We better give Sparky a moment."

I cry like a baby until no tears are left, and the room is dark with the approach of night. From the other room, I hear Nash's gentle voice and Ambrose's faint coos and giggles for awhile before the cabin falls silent.

Embarrassment, shame, and guilt grip me. I should've known better than to give him the noodles. Or not been so distracted by Nash during our meal that I could have paid closer attention to the baby.

All I know is I'm not cut out to be a nanny, and I'm not fooling anyone by living in a house with a man who fills my head with deliciously dangerous thoughts. I'm in over my head, and I'm finally willing to admit it. Mama and Daddy's plane ticket offer suddenly sounds more than tempting.

The thought of leaving Nash and Ambrose tugs at my heart. But maybe it's better this way. After all, Ambrose deserves a real caretaker who's not going to let anything happen to him. And nothing good can come from Nash and me pretending we're something we aren't in the cozy depths of this cabin.

I stir quietly, turning on the lights in my bedroom and straightening the blankets and sheets. I put my luggage on the bed, preparing to dig into drawers and pack up. But first, I have to make sure Ambrose is okay. If I can be trusted with such responsibilities.

Chapter Thirteen

NASH

A mbrose snoozes in the swing as I sit at the kitchen table, nursing my second glass of wine. The bedroom door squeaks open, and soft footfalls pad my way, stopping at the entry to the kitchen.

I look up at Naomi, admiring the way the light from the kitchen makes her long curls golden like an angel's. Her cheeks glow, ruddy from crying, and her pretty sky-blue eyes are red. She looks nervously from me to Ambrose and back again, her bottom lip and chin quivering as she eyes the baby.

Naomi swipes the backs of her hands over her cheeks as a new onslaught of tears grips her, and I can't take it anymore. I stand, sauntering in her direction and pulling her into my arms. "Shh, darling, it's going to be okay. We all just had a little scare, but Ambrose is fine. We're all fine."

"B-b-but," she sputters against my chest, causing warm waves to radiate and swirl around my heart. "But what if he wasn't okay?" she squeaks, tipping her head up to eye me gravely. "I should've never given him noodles. Or been distracted from watching him."

Naomi pulls away from me, striding into the living room.

I follow her, my mind racing, trying to find the right words to calm the stormy woman.

"Sparky," I croon, grabbing her from behind and wrapping my arms around her. "There's nothing you could have done differently. Babies choke sometimes, whether they're human, cow, or horse. It happens. And he's fine now. We're fine."

"But I'm not cut out for this, Nash." She sobs. "If anything happened to Ambrose, I couldn't live with myself. Honestly, I'm scared, and I don't know what I'm doing."

"You're scared because this is scary. But you do know what you're doing. I've seen you with Ambrose, and he loves you." *I love you.* I bite my tongue, straining not to say what I feel with my whole heart.

"Don't you get it?" she says, pulling away and heading towards the bedroom again. I follow, stopping her before she can slam the door on me. "I've never cared for my own baby before. I don't know the first thing about it except what I remember from my younger siblings. I've been thinking about it, and you're both better off without me. I mean, who am I kidding? What am I thinking? I'm not cut out for any of this."

She enters the bedroom, and I follow, a thick knot lodging in my throat even as she throws her hands up, going on and on about her ineptitude. My eyes settle on the bed and her open suitcase and carry-on. She's packing. Naomi is leaving me for good. My heart shudders at the thought, and the backs of my eyes sting dangerously.

But anger grips me, driving my next words and making my voice shake. "Are you abandoning me and Ambrose? After little more than a day?"

"I've been thinking it through, and you both will be better without me. Ambrose deserves a real nanny. One trained in CPR and all the things. One that won't make stupid mistakes." Her bottom lip trembles, and her eyes simmer with guilt.

"You can't leave me," I plead. I've never spoken to a woman this way before. "I need you, Naomi."

She pulls away, turning her back on me. A scowl captures her face, her movements jerky and angry as she returns to packing. "You can do better than me, and you will do better than me. I should've never taken this job, but I ..." Naomi eyes me guiltily.

"But what?"

She shakes her head.

I step forward, pulling her back towards me and snagging her chin to make her look up into my eyes. "But what?" I repeat.

"But I wanted more time with you to try to figure out why I feel these uncontrollable feelings for you. Even though I don't want to. Even though I know they're wrong."

My heart hammers against my ribs. "What feelings, Naomi?"

She shakes her head, looking away.

"Sparky?"

Her cerulean eyes flash towards mine, her face flushed. "It doesn't matter because it could never work out between us anyway. All the more reason I shouldn't be living with you like we're married. We can say that's not what we're doing, but it is. And I've never done anything like this with any man. They've all been so easy to resist. Why do you have to be different? Why do you have to make everything so difficult for me?"

"Darling," I say, staring long and hard at her, too many emotions swirling inside for me to quantify. I bite my bottom lip, breathing harder. "Darling—" I repeat, trailing off again. It's as if I'm stuck mid-thought and can't move past it.

Naomi knits her brows, scrutinizing my expression.

I lick my bottom lip, grimacing and shifting my weight.

I'm stuck somewhere between pained and perplexed with a world of need devouring me whole.

"How do I say this?" I mutter almost more to myself than her.

"Nash, you're scaring me. What is it?" Her wide blue eyes echo her concern.

I swallow loudly. Time to cowboy up, as Rugged would say. "If you're worried about the marrying part, don't. I'd marry you in a heartbeat. I mean, I will marry you as soon as possible. As soon as Colorado will allow if you'll have me."

She blinks at me slowly as if she's unable to process what I'm saying. As if she understands it, but she doesn't get it. My eyes dig soul-deep into her, desperate for any favorable indication that she likes my offer.

I add, grabbing her hand and pressing it to my chest so she can feel my heart beating. "I'm sorry I don't have a ring yet because this has all kind of caught me off guard. But I have started looking online. And this next weekend, we can go jewelry shopping in Ouray or Telluride to see if you find something you like?"

Her mouth hangs open, and my heart kathunks in my chest.

Silence. I can't take another stitch of this infernal quiet or Naomi's unreadable countenance.

My face hardens, and I clench my jaw. Narrowing my eyes, I plead, "You need to say something, Naomi, because you've really left me hanging here, and it's paining my heart something awful."

Tears well in her sweet gaze, her face torn. Looking back towards the kitchen and Ambrose and then up at me, she says, "But I almost jus—"

"Nah, nah, nah," I interrupt, my voice raw. "You didn't almost do anything. The kid choked himself, and he's bound to do it again, darling. Life is fatal for everyone who's ever participated. But your job is to love him no matter what, despite the fear of loss. To be brave and take that risk. Just like I'm asking you to take it with me. Because I don't want to be a ramblin' man anymore. And being with you like this, getting a taste of domesticity with the most beautiful, caring, amazing, tender woman I've ever met, has me hopelessly addicted. There are no lengths I won't go to, to preserve and cultivate whatever's happening between us. But I need you to want it, too."

"Nash—"

I cut her off with my lips, kissing her passionately. She tastes and feels like everything I've ever wanted. Everything I didn't think I had a right to want, let alone claim. "You can't leave me, Naomi. Not after what I asked you. Well, I mean, you can if you don't love me—" I stop mid-sentence, feeling sucker punched. "Look what you've done to me, Sparky? I'm saying stuff I've never said to any woman before."

Her cheeks burn, and her eyes wash over me with the warmest, sweetest affection. She welcomes my words, though a sliver of doubt still colors her voice. "But I feel like such a failure. I'm afraid to be alone in the same room with Ambrose now. What if I mess up again?"

I palm her cheeks, tears filling my eyes. "You will mess up, and so will I. But you can't give up on love ... on family because of fear of losing each other. Naomi Donovan, I love you, and the idea of trying to live without you ... well, it's unthinkable." As I say the words, a lightbulb goes off in my head. Everything Rugged said to me earlier in the stables suddenly makes sense.

"I never want to hurt Ambrose, and I never want to hurt you, Nash."

"But?" I question, deepening the creases in my forehead.

"There's no 'but,'" she squeaks. "Because as reckless as this sounds, I love baby Ambrose..."

My brows arch, my face tightening.

"And I love you."

My heart explodes, and fireworks go off in my head. "Thank God," I exclaim, pulling her into my arms and pressing my cheek to her head. "Are you saying what I think you're saying?"

"That I'll marry you?" Naomi clarifies.

I pull back, eyeing her apprehensively. Tears moisten the blonde Okie's soft cheeks.

"Yes, Nash Carter, I will marry you, which means you better be on your best behavior until then." She grabs my hands, pulling them up from where they've strayed and back to the tops of her hips.

My mouth crashes into hers, my kiss reckless and untamed. Naomi's hands come up to my neck, encircling it, and she returns my embrace passionately until I feel heated sparks to the tips of my toes. I lift her off the ground, squeezing her desperately.

My thoughts feel inarticulate, a noisy jumble as I set her feet back on the ground. "So, you're not going to leave me, then?" I ask, furrowing my brows, my voice dark with emotion.

"I don't want to leave you or Ambrose—"

"Then, don't. Ever."

"But how can you be so sure about us?" she asks, knitting her brows. "I watched your rodeoing videos earlier and the parade of gorgeous women never far from your side. How could you want an Okie bumpkin when you could have your choice of dressed-to-the-nines, perfectly groomed rodeo queens?"

"I told you this before, Sparky. You're one-of-a-kind. There's not a woman who's your equal. Who holds even half a candle to you. I can't live without you. Even if it means facing my fears about not being good enough and abandonment and all my other issues. If I haven't made myself clear yet, Sparky. You are the only woman who's ever made me feel this way, and whoever will."

"Then, I better stay right here with you," she says in an adorable little voice that ignites the blaze afresh in my heart. "Because I feel the same way. I don't want to think about living without you."

"Thank God," I whisper, kissing the crown of her head.

"Do we have to have a big shebang like Luna and Ledger? Or can we elope?" she asks breathlessly.

I'm stunned yet again at how she reads my thoughts and shares my desires. I confess, "I'd marry you today if I could. But I'm fine with an elopement if you are because, dang girl, I don't want to wait to make you my wife."

Naomi smiles so broadly that the skin around her eyes crinkles, and her cheeks flush. "I don't need a big fancy wedding, cowboy. I need you. But there is the matter of convincing my parents that what we're doing is right."

"Leave your dad to me," I say with a firm nod.

"Best of luck to you," my Okie replies sassily, a challenge in her voice that fills me with apprehension. But I know in my heart everything will work out. I'll do whatever it takes to win over her parents and show them I'm worthy of their drop-dead gorgeous, sharp-tongued, big-hearted, perfect daughter.

Epilogue

NAOMI

ONE MONTH LATER

"Alright, Daddy, you can open your eyes," I say to Nash, seated dutifully at the table with closed lids. The handsome cowboy who now wears my golden band on his left-hand stares at the breakfast feast in front of him, eyeing it hungrily.

"Get over here," he says in a gently scolding tone to me.

I stride toward him, and he pulls me unceremoniously into his lap, kissing me breathless and fingering my matching gold band with intricate vine work and tiny inlaid diamonds.

He tangles his fingers with mine. "Wife, you've outdone yourself."

"Ambrose helped me," I tease, looking towards the adorable golden-haired baby in the high chair next to us.

"Nice work, buckaroo," he says in cheerful tones as I hand Nash a card with "Tex" on the envelope.

He opens it, tears filling his eyes as he peruses the Father's Day card inside, reading the words carefully. He swipes the back of his hand quickly over his cheeks, smiling broadly before lavishing me in more kisses.

"Thank you, wife," he says in grumbly tones, capturing my lips again before turning to Ambrose and thanking him, too. The little guy blows raspberries his way, and we all chuckle together.

Arching his eyebrow, the rugged cowboy looks at me with a suddenly grave face. "Speaking of parenting, I received a call from CPS."

My heart immediately pounds in my chest, my throat tightens, and my mouth goes dry. My worst fear is that Nell will reappear out of the blue, demanding Ambrose as though Nash and I have been nothing more than an extended babysitting service. I wouldn't be able to sleep at night knowing the woman who abandoned him without a second thought controls his future once more. My voice quivers as I ask, "And?"

"And," Nash says, eyeing Ambrose pensively. "They tracked my sister down through my grandparents. A little financial maneuvering, and she's ready to sign over parental rights if we would like to formally adopt Ambrose."

I blink slowly a couple of times, my heart overflowing with joy as I process his words.

He holds up a hand. "Now, I want you to give it some serious thought, Sparky. Because I know as much as you've enjoyed helping out with the little guy, you also can't wait to start our own family. And juggling two babies at the same time is probably more than any woman wants to entertain."

"What about mothers of twins?" I ask, my mind already made up.

Nash chuckles, shaking his head. "You yourself said twins run in your family, so we might get more than we wish for anyway. I wouldn't fault you one bit if you feel Ambrose is too—"

I cut my husband off with a passionate kiss, melting into his embrace. His lips cover mine enthusiastically, delicious sparks sizzling between us as his tongue swipes into my mouth, claiming me. My heart pounds as my fingers tangle into his hair, dissolving any and all hesitation in my husband's frame. His shoulders relax, and he moans happily.

Pulling back, I say breathlessly, stroking his handsome bearded cheeks and making a scratchy noise, "Ambrose is a part of our family, baby. I can't imagine life without him. Can you?"

Nash's eyes sparkle with a mixture of happiness and relief. Staring at the infant happily slapping the high chair tray, he admits, " Thank God. Because in answer to your question. No, I can't imagine my life without him or you. Geez, what have you two done to me in a little over a month?" The rawness edging his words tells me how sincere they are.

"Turned you into the best daddy in the world," I giggle as he nuzzles my cheek.

"I hope I'm a decent husband, too?" he asks in rich, deep tones, tracing the shell of my ear with his lips and tongue.

Desire thickens my throat, and I swallow hard, attempting to think and speak. "I don't want to over-inflate your ego, cowboy. But you are the absolute best husband ever put on this planet."

"Oh, yeah?" he whispers, tracing the line of my jaw in featherlight kisses that end at the cleft of my chin. "And how do you know that for sure?"

"Because you bring me wildflowers every afternoon when you get home from work. And you have a million poetic things to say to me, an extravagant compliment always at the ready," I gasp as his fingertips graze teasingly over my collarbones and neck, lighting sparks along my trembling flesh. "You protect and care for me in every way, and you make me feel safer, more understood, and seen than any person ever has.

You finish my sentences for me, read my thoughts, and love me more fiercely than I ever dreamed possible."

"Wait," he says in teasing tones. "I don't like what you said." His voice has a flirtatious tone to it.

"And why not, Mr. Carter?"

"Because, Mrs. Carter, you stole everything straight out of my head that I feel about you. Well, except for the part about the flowers and poetry. I'm definitely the flower wrangler and wordsmith in this family."

I giggle, heady warmth filling my core as he continues showering my face and neck in kisses.

"Agreed. You are most assuredly the cowboy poet in the family," I concede.

"And you're the amazing cook. So, we're pretty much even in that regard."

"Glad to know I'm holding up my end of the bargain," I tease.

He leans back slightly, leveling his gaze on me, his eyes red with emotion. "Holding up your end of the bargain? No, Sparky, you're so much more than that. You're my *everything*. The living, breathing heart and soul of this home. God's greatest gift to me. You've taught me what it means to love and trust and given me the family I've always wanted. I love you, wife."

Tears blur my vision as I whisper, kissing his cheek, "And I love you, Nash Carter, more than I ever thought possible. Forever."

~

If you loved Naomi & Nash's romance in *Rule #3 Dad Knows Best*, then you'll love
Allison & Max's story in
Rule #4 Be a Good Fake Wife.

CHECK IT OUT HERE

Find all the books in the Rules for Dating a Single Dad series at:

RULES FOR DATING A SINGLE DAD

~

Did you enjoy *Rule #3 Dad Knows Best?* If so, please review this book on Amazon, Goodreads, and Bookbub. Your feedback is greatly appreciated!

Amazon
Goodreads
Bookbub

Let's stay in touch! You can sign up for my newsletter at **ebsilva.com,** and be sure to follow me on Amazon for news about upcoming books and my latest releases: **amazon.com/ author/ebsilva**

Also by E.B. Silva

Mistletoe Mismatch - Worlds collide mile-high in Colorado when a blizzard traps Chase Heart, a single dad and widower who's given up on love, with Chanel Love, a jaded romance writer who wants to believe in forever. Can a little Christmas magic prove this mismatch is made in heaven?

My Starry Valentine - Wilderness watercolorist, Luna Solace, couldn't be more different than Ledger Brooks, a grumpy mountain man, wounded warrior, and astronomer. Yet, a tender promise in her eyes, rivaling the beauty of celestial bodies, makes him wonder if their love might be written in the stars...

Rule #2 Keep Calm and Carry On - What happens when a cowboy with a gentle soul meets a mom who's afraid to love again? He rescued her on a muddy backroad... Now he might just rescue her heart.

About the Author

E.B. Silva writes sweet, clean contemporary romances with all the feels. Her stories feature gruff cowboys and mountain men and the sassy, quirky woman they fall head over heels for.

Favorite tropes include grumpy/sunshine, fake engagement, marriage of convenience, found family, and best friends to lovers.

If you like cozy small-town vibes, expansive mountain views, and lovable characters who always find happily ever afters with their soulmates, E.B. Silva's your girl. Satisfying, heartfelt HEAs guaranteed!

Head to E.B. Silva's website to never miss out on upcoming and new releases as well as freebies and deals: www.ebsilva.com.

- instagram.com/authorebsilva
- tiktok.com/@authorebsilva
- facebook.com/authorebsilva
- amazon.com/author/ebsilva
- bookbub.com/books/my-starry-valentine-a-sweet-ex-military-mountain-man-romance-by-e-b-silva